厉以宁·著

吴浩·编

彭琳·译

诗词选

·汉英对照·

四川人民出版社

图书在版编目（CIP）数据

厉以宁诗词选：汉英对照 / 厉以宁著；吴浩编；彭琳译. -- 成都：四川人民出版社，2020.11
ISBN 978-7-220-11989-7

Ⅰ.①厉… Ⅱ.①厉…②吴…③彭… Ⅲ.①诗词—作品集—中国—当代—汉、英 Ⅳ.①I227

中国版本图书馆CIP数据核字（2020）第168492号

LIYINING SHICI XUAN
HANYING DUIZHAO

厉以宁诗词选：汉英对照

厉以宁 著 吴浩 编 彭琳 译

责任编辑	张春晓 王雪
封面设计	李其飞
版式设计	戴雨虹
责任印制	祝健
出版发行	四川人民出版社（成都市槐树街2号）
网　　址	http://www.scpph.com
E-mail	scrmcbs@sina.com
新浪微博	@四川人民出版社
微信公众号	四川人民出版社
发行部业务电话	（028）86259624　86259453
防盗版举报电话	（028）86259624
照　　排	四川胜翔数码印务设计有限公司
印　　刷	成都东江印务有限公司
成品尺寸	145mm×210mm
印　　张	8.25
字　　数	120千
版　　次	2020年11月第1版
印　　次	2020年11月第1次印刷
书　　号	ISBN 978-7-220-11989-7
定　　价	58.00元

■版权所有·侵权必究

本书若出现印装质量问题，请与我社发行部联系调换
电话：（028）86259453

2008年，正值我和何玉春金婚纪念之际，商务印书馆出版了《厉以宁诗词选集》，收录我1947—2007年间创作的诗词666首。时隔十二年，四川人民出版社准备出版《厉以宁诗词选》汉英对照本，我委托吴浩先生从商务印书馆出版的《厉以宁诗词选集》中选出部分作品，并加上后期创作的一些诗作，共108首，编成此书，供诗词爱好者们阅读。入选本书的作品创作时间跨度为1947—2017年。

——厉以宁

◎ 相见欢
仪征新城途中，
1947
002

Tune: Meeting in Delight
—— During a journey to Xincheng, Yizheng, 1947
003

◎ 木兰花
偕黄业耘表兄游杭州西湖，1948
004

Tune: Magnolia
—Touring West Lake in Hangzhou with my cousin Huang Yeyun, 1948
005

◎ 如梦令
沅陵麻溪铺，1949
006

Tune: Dreamlike Song
—Maxipu, Yuanling, 1949
007

◎ 浣溪沙
重游沅陵桃溪坪，1949
008

Tune: Silk-washing Stream
—Revisiting Taoxiping in Yuanling, 1949
009

◎ 七绝
湖南泸溪，1949
010

A Seven-character Quatrain
—Luxi, Hunan, 1949
011

- 南歌子
  山溪，1950
  012

Tune: A Southern Song
—Mountain streams, 1950
013

- 钗头凤
  湘西，山行，1951
  014

Tune: Phoenix Hairpin
—A mountain trip in western Hunan, 1951
015

- 南乡子
  湖南益阳渡口，1951
  016

Tune: Song of a Southern Country
—At the ferry in Yiyang, Hunan, 1951
017

- 诉衷情
  在长沙接到北京大学录取通知书有感，1951
  018

A Confession
—Receiving Peking University Letter of Admission in Changsha, 1951
019

- 菩萨蛮
  别长沙，1951
  020

Tune: Buddha-like Dancers
—Farewell to Changsha, 1951
021

- 柳梢青
  北京大学沙滩校园白楼法学院图书馆，1951
  022

Tune: Green Willow Twigs
— Written at the Law School Library in the White Building of Peking University, Shatan Section, 1951
023

卜算子
冬至日，偕赵辉杰、马雍散步从沙滩到安定门外，1951
024

Tune: Song of Divination
—On Winter Solstice Day, walking with Zhao Huijie and Ma Yong from Shatan to Andingmenwai, 1951
025

减字木兰花
北河沿，春节，1952
026

Tune: Magnolia in Shortened Form
—Beiheyan, Spring Festival, 1952
027

西江月
路过海淀冰窖胡同，1952
028

Tune: The Moon over the West River
—Passing Bingjiao Hutong in Haidian district, 1952
029

桃源忆故人
北京大学迁到西郊后遇见中学同学姚子范，1952
030

Thinking of an Old Friend in Taoyuan
—Meeting my middle-school fellow Yao Zifan after Peking University moved to the western suburb, 1952
031

采桑子
颐和园，1953
032

Tune: Picking Mulberries
—The Summer Palace, 1953
033

十六字令
无题，1954
034

A Sixteen-word Song
—No title, 1954
035

减字木兰花
陪赵迺抟老师、骆涵素师母游香山，1955
036

Tune: Magnolia in Shortened Form
—Touring Fragrant Hills with my teacher Zhao Naituan and his wife Luo Hansu, 1955
037

鹧鸪天
大学毕业自勉，1955
038

Tune: Partridge Sky
—A self-encouraging poem written upon university graduation, 1955
039

七绝
重读周邦彦词，1956
040

A Seven-character Quatrain
—Rereading the *ci*-lyrics of Zhou Bangyan, 1965
041

浣溪沙
为何玉春题照，1957
042

Tune: Silk-washing Stream
—Written for He Yuchun's photo, 1957
043

五绝
无题，1957
044

A Five-character Quatrain
—No title, 1957
045

- 浣溪沙
  除夕，1958
  046

- 人月圆
  题结婚照，1958
  048

- 天仙子
  送赵辉杰赴兰州，1958
  050

- 踏莎行
  斋堂，修渠，1958
  052

- 采桑子
  灵山脚下，夜宿农家，1958
  054

- 浣溪沙
  无题，1959
  056

- Tune: Silk-washing Stream
  —On Lunar New Year's Eve, 1958
  047

- Tune: The Full Moon
  —A poem for our wedding photo, 1958
  049

- Tune: Song of Immortals
  —Seeing Zhao Huijie Off to Lanzhou, 1958
  051

- Tune: Treading on Grass
  —Repairing a ditch at Zhaitang, 1958
  053

- Tune: Picking Mulberries
  —Sleeping in a farmer's house under the foot of Lingshan Mountain, 1958
  055

- Tune: Silk-washing Stream
  —No title, 1959
  057

鹊桥仙
三十岁生日，独自骑车游圆明园遗址，
1960
058

Tune: Immortals on the Magpie Bridge
—Written upon my 30th birthday, riding alone to Yuanmingyuan Park, 1960
059

南乡子
记厉放患麻疹并发肺炎，何玉春连夜自鞍山赶回北京，
1962
060

Tune: Song of a Southern Country
—Lines composed to mark He Yuchun's coming to Beijing from Anshan the very night when Li Fang was down with measles and pneumonia, 1962
061

浣溪沙
无题，1962
062

Tune: Silk-washing Stream
—No title, 1962
063

鹧鸪天
中秋，1963
064

Tune: Partridge Sky
—Middle Autumn, 1963
065

七绝
咏梅（窗前一株梅树，与我作伴已数年），1964
066

A Seven-character Quatrain
—To the old plum tree in front of my window,
1964
067

◈ 调笑令
记厉伟学步，
1964
068

Tune: Song of Flirtation
—A poem for Li Wei learning to walk, 1964
069

◈ 浪淘沙
船过湖北嘉鱼赤壁，
1964
070

Tune: Sand-sifting Waves
—Passing Red Cliff in the county of Jiayu in Hubei by boat, 1964
071

◈ 南乡子
湖北江陵城外所见，
1964
072

Tune: Song of a Southern Country
—Outside the city of Jiangling, Hubei, 1964
073

◈ 朝中措
湖北江陵滩桥，
春节，
1965
074

Tune: Measures at Court
—At Tanqiao in Jiangling, Hubei in the 1965 Spring Festival, 1965
075

◈ 柳梢青
带厉放、厉伟散步到北京海淀六郎庄，
1965
076

Tune: Green Willow Twigs
—Walking with Li Fang and Li Wei to Liulangzhuang in Haidian district, 1965
077

忆秦娥
北京建国门桥头，1965
078

Tune: Thinking of a Qin Lady
—On Jianguomen Bridge, Beijing, 1965
079

破阵子
昌平北太平庄，1968
080

Tune: Dance of the Calvary
—Beitaipingzhuang, Changping, 1968
081

昭君怨
去江西途中，车过杭州，天已黑，先雨后晴，一夜难眠，1969
082

Tune: Zhaojun's Complain
—Passing Hangzhou on my Jiangxi-bound journey, a sleepless night after rain, 1969
083

七绝
在鲤鱼洲度过39岁生日，1969
084

A Seven-character Quatrain
—Spending my 39th birthday in Liyuzhou, 1969
085

七古
鲤鱼洲上所见，1970
086

A Seven-character Rhymed Poem
—What I saw in Liyuzhou, 1970
087

浣溪沙
中秋节，于鲤鱼洲，1970
088

Tune: Silk-washing Stream
—Mid-Autumn in Liyuzhou, 1970
089

相见欢
四十自述，1970
090

Tune: Meeting in Delight
—A self-account upon my 40th birthday, 1970
091

鹧鸪天
迎何玉春来鲤鱼洲，1971
092

Tune: Partridge Sky
—Reuniting with He Yuchun in Liyuzhou, 1971
093

鹧鸪天
赠何玉春，鲤鱼洲，1971
094

Tune: Partridge Sky
—A poem for He Yuchun written in Liyuzhou, 1971
095

七律
四十五岁生日，于大兴县农村，1975
096

A Seven-character Regulated Verse
—Written upon my 45th birthday at a village in Daxing county, 1975
097

采桑子
北京一月街景，1976
098

Tune: Picking Mulberries
—Beijing in January, a street scene, 1976
099

调笑令
送厉放到昌平马池口公社西坨村插队，1977
100

Tune: Song of Flirtation
—Sending Li Fang to work in Xituo village, Machikou Commune in Changping, 1977
101

❖ 南歌子
元旦有感，
1979
102

Tune: A Southern Song
—Lines composed on New Year's Day, 1979
103

❖ 七绝
由北京赴杭州，车过
安徽凤阳，1979
104

A Seven-character Quatrain
—Journey from Beijing to Hangzhou, bypassing Fengyang in Anhui, 1979
105

❖ 七绝
无题，1980
106

A Seven-character Quatrain
—No title, 1980
107

❖ 南乡子
五十岁生日，1980
108

Tune: Song of a Southern Country
—Composed on my 50th birthday, 1980
109

❖ 鹧鸪天
游四川青城山有感，
1981
110

Tune: Partridge Sky
—Touring Mount Qingchen in Sichuan, 1981
111

鹧鸪天
为厉伟考取北京大学化学系而作，1981
112

Tune: Partridge Sky
—Composed upon Li Wei's admission to the Chemistry Department of Peking University, 1981
113

南歌子
游漓江，1982
114

Tune: A Southern Song
—Touring Lijiang River, 1982
115

菩萨蛮
黄山归来，1984
116

Tune: Buddha-like Dancers
—Returning from Mount Huangshan, 1984
117

鹧鸪天
为厉放获得硕士学位作，1985
118

Tune: Partridge Sky
—In celebration of Li Fang obtaining Master's Degree, 1985
119

浣溪沙
由大连乘轮船到塘沽，1985
120

Tune: Silk-washing Stream
—Journey from Dalian to Tanggu by ship, 1985
121

踏莎行
于北京大学图书馆整理文稿，1987
122

Tune: Treading on Grass
—Preparing a manuscript at Peking University Library, 1987
123

南歌子
为北京大学经济管理系干部班毕业而作，1987
124

Tune: A Southern Song
—Upon completion of the Cadre Class of Peking University Economic Management Department, 1987
125

鹊桥仙
看电视剧《红楼梦》，咏贾宝玉，1987
126

Tune: Immortals on the Magpie Bridge
—A poem for Jia Baoyu, 1987
127

唐多令
看电视剧《红楼梦》，咏林黛玉，1987
128

Tune: Tang Duo Song
—A poem for Lin Daiyu, 1987
129

减字木兰花
看电视剧《红楼梦》，咏薛宝钗，1987
130

Tune: Magnolia in Shortened Form
—A poem for Xue Baochai, 1987
131

苏幕遮
看电视剧《红楼梦》，咏探春，1987
132

Tune: Waterbag Dance
—A poem for Tanchun, 1987
133

巫山一段云
看电视剧《红楼梦》，咏史湘云，1987
134

Tune: Cloud on Mount Wu
—A poem for Shi Xiangyun, 1987
135

少年游
看电视剧《红楼梦》大结局，再咏贾宝玉，1987
136

Tune: Wandering While Young
—Another poem for Jia Baoyu, composed after watching the end of the TV series *The Dream of the Red Mansion*, 1987
137

卜算子
年终自叙，1987
138

Tune: Song of Divination
—A self-account at year's end, 1987
139

七古
长沙，湘江桥头，1988
140

A Seven-character Rhymed Poem in Ancient Style
—Xiangjiang Bridge, Changsha, 1988
141

木兰花
悼念岳母，记1953年送走二女玉春后，岳母独自留在沅陵家中之事，1988
142

Tune: Magnolia
—A lament to Mother-in-law, who lived alone in Yuanling after sending off her second daughter Yuchun in 1953, 1988
143

忆秦娥
江苏淮安宝应途中所见，1989
146

Tune: Thinking of a Qin Lady
—What I saw in Baoying, Huai'an during my journey in Jiangsu, 1989
147

浣溪沙
六十自述，1990
148

Tune: Silk-washing Stream
—A self-account at the age of 60, 1990
149

七律
甘肃酒泉左公柳碑前，1991
150

A Seven-character Regulated Verse
—Before the tabular of Zuo Zongtang in Jiuquan, Gansu, 1991
151

七律
从图书馆借得王沂孙《碧山乐府》，读后有感，1991
152

A Seven-character Regulated Verse
—Reading *Collected Poems of Green Mountains* by Wang Yisun, borrowed from the library, 1991
153

七律
虎门炮台，1992
154

A Seven-character Regulated Verse
—Humen Port, 1992
155

七律
湖南芷江抗战胜利受降纪念碑坊，1992
156

A Seven-character Regulated Verse
—A memorial arch of Japanese surrender in Zhijiang, Hunan, 1992
157

鹧鸪天
游浙江定海普陀山，船中闻邻座几位民营企业家闲谈有感，1993
158

Tune: Partridge Sky
—Touring Mount Putuo in Zhejiang by boat, overhearing several private entrepreneurs' casual talk, 1993
159

减字木兰花
—— 结婚三十六周年，在海南三亚，1994
160

Tune: Magnolia in Shortened Form
—Commemorating the 36th wedding anniversary in Sanya, Hainan, 1994
161

南歌子
母亲去世后整理旧相册，翻到我婴儿100天时的照片，伤感万分，1995
162

Tune: A Southern Song
—Sorting out an old album after Mother's death, immensely sick at heart when seeing my 100-day photo, 1995
163

渔歌子
福建泰宁，1996
164

Tune: A Fisherman's Song
—Taining, Fujian, 1996
165

- 唐多令
  过河南朱仙镇，1996
  166

  Tune: Tang Duo Song
  —Passing Zhuxian county in Henan, 1996
  167

- 调笑令
  为厉澳两周岁题照，1997
  168

  Tune: Song of Flirtation
  —A poem for Li Ao's 2nd birthday photo, 1997
  169

- 南乡子
  为母亲扫墓，1997
  170

  Tune: Song of a Southern Country
  —Sweeping Mother's tomb, 1997
  171

- 减字木兰花
  贺厉放获博士学位，1998
  172

  Tune: Magnolia in Shortened Form
  —In congratulation of Li Fang obtaining a doctorial degree, 1998
  173

- 钗头凤
  记厉莎周岁，1999
  174

  Tune: Phoenix Hairpin
  —In celebration of Li Sha's first birthday, 1999
  175

- 破阵子
  七十感怀，2000
  176

  Tune: Dance of the Calvary
  —Written upon my 70th birthday, 2000
  177

- 柳梢青
  过宁夏固原有感，2002
  178

- 鹧鸪天
  瑞士洛桑古迹，2002
  180

- 鹧鸪天
  回鞍山，代何玉春作，2003
  182

- 洞仙歌
  为厉放四十五岁、厉伟四十岁而作，2003
  184

- 虞美人
  山东荣成市成山头，2004
  188

- 清平乐
  甘肃崆峒山，2004
  190

- Tune: Green Willow Twigs
  —Passing Guyuan in Ningxia, 2002
  179

- Tune: Partridge Sky
  —Historical site of Lausanne, Sweden, 2002
  181

- Tune: Partridge Sky
  —Returning to Anshan, written on behalf of He Yuchun, 2003
  183

- Tune: Song of a Fairy in the Cave
  —Written upon Li Fang's 45th and Li Wei's 40th birthdays, 2003
  185

- Tune: The Beautiful Lady Yu
  —At Chengshantou in Rongcheng, Shandong, 2004
  189

- Tune: Pure Serene Music
  —Kongtong Mountain, Gansu, 2004
  191

踏莎行
重到济南，2004
192

Tune: Treading on Grass
—Revisiting Jinan, 2004
193

七律
从教五十周年暨七十五岁生日自叙，2005
194

A Seven-character Regulated Verse
—A self-account on the 50th anniversary of my teaching career & 75th birthday, 2005
195

踏莎行
江西婺源农村所见，2006
196

Tune: Treading on Grass
—A view of the countryside in Wuyuan, Jiangxi, 2006
197

一剪梅
结婚四十九年，代何玉春作，2007
198

Tune: A Twig of Plum Blossoms
—The 49th wedding anniversary, written on behalf of He Yuchun, 2007
199

满庭芳
北京大学110周年校庆，2008
200

Tune: Courtyard Full of Fragrance
—In celebration of Peking University's 110th anniversary, 2008
201

清平乐
记慧慧、嘉嘉100
天，2008
204

Tune: Pure Serene Music
—Lines composed to mark Huihui and
Jiajia being 100 days old, 2008
205

七绝
内蒙乌拉特中旗秦长
城遗址，2009
206

A Seven-character Quatrain
—The site of Qin-state Great Wall in Urad
Middle Banner in Inner Mongolia, 2009
207

木兰花
题重庆市武隆县仙女
山镇，2010
208

Tune: Magnolia
—Fairy Mountain town in Wulong county,
Chongqing, 2010
209

七绝
烟台养马岛，秦始皇
东巡时将此岛辟为养
马场，2010
210

A Seven-character Quatrain
—Horse Island in Yantai, which
Qinshihuang reserved for horse-keeping
during his eastward journey, 2010
211

浣溪沙
莎士比亚故居（英国
牛津郡莎士比亚故
居，遇见外地来此演
出的小剧团），2012
212

Tune: Silk-washing Stream
—Meeting a non-local troupe at
Shakespeare's former residence in Oxford,
2012
213

- 七绝
  为北京大学光华管理
  学院校友返校日作，
  2012
  214

  A Seven-character Quatrain
  —Lines composed on Guanghua College
  of Peking University Alumni Day, 2012
  215

- 踏莎行
  第七次赴贵州毕节扶
  贫有感，2012
  216

  Tune: Treading on Grass
  —Lines composed upon my 7th journey
  to Bijie in Guizhou under the anti-poverty
  programme, 2012
  217

- 鹧鸪天
  四川广安邓小平故
  里，2013
  218

  Tune: Partridge Sky
  —Guang'an, hometown of Deng Xiaoping,
  2013
  219

- 七绝
  三清山，2014
  220

  A Seven-character Quatrain
  —Sanqing Mountain, 2014
  221

- 鹧鸪天
  《厉以宁诗词全集》
  整理完毕，有感而
  作，2017
  222

  Tune: Partridge Sky
  —Upon completion of *The Complete
  Poetry of Li Yining*, 2017
  223

洙泗濠濮，松柏桐椿（编后记）
——记厉以宁著作外译，并祝先生九秩寿辰　224

厉以宁诗选

The Selected Poetry
by Li Yining

相见欢
仪征新城途中，1947

桨声篙影波纹，

石桥礅，

蚕豆花开一路水乡春。

长跳板，

小河岸，

洗衣人。

绿裤红衫都道是新婚。

注：

江苏仪征是作者的故乡。新城当时是仪征的一个小镇，距仪征东门约5公里。1947年4月，作者当时是金陵中学高中二年级学生，放春假期间，特地由南京回到故乡仪征，住在小姑母家中。

Tune: Meeting in Delight

—During a journey to Xincheng, Yizheng, 1947

Paddling sound, pole shadow, water waves,

Stone bridge piers,

The springtime watertown is aglow with broad bean flowers.

Long is the board,

Small the riverside,

Where a girl launders,

In trousers green and a coat red, said to be newlywed.

Note:

Yizheng in Jiangsu province is the author's hometown. At the time Xincheng was a small town about five kilometers to the East Gate of Yizheng. The author was then a second-year senior-high-school student at Jinling Middle School, Nanjing. During his spring vacation, he went his way from Nanjing to Yizheng for a short stay with his younger aunt.

木兰花
偕黄业耘表兄游杭州西湖，1948

花丛柳岸灯明灭，
几处秋虫声切切，
晚来缓步过苏堤，
桥下清波明似雪。

难消倦意当休歇，
架上闲书随手阅，
钱塘遗事早茫茫，
只见飞来峰外月。

注：

1948年秋，作者和表兄黄业耘第一次来杭州，有感而作。

Tune: Magnolia

—Touring West Lake in Hangzhou with my cousin Huang Yeyun, 1948

Amidst flowers and across willows flickers the light,

Here and there crickets chirp faint but tight.

When night comes I stroll along the Su Causeway,

Beneath the bridge the river looks snow bright.

It's time to stay, when in vain weariness to fight,

Casually browse a book off the shelf as you might.

Dim and vague for long is the past of River Qiantang,

Only the moon beyond the Flying Peak comes to sight.

Note:

In the autumn of 1948, the author went to Hangzhou with his cousin Huang Yeyun for the first time. This poem was specially written for that occasion.

如梦令
沅陵麻溪铺，1949

残雪东风吹去，
四月村村盼雨，
心急似燃烧，
忽见山头云聚。
来雨！
来雨！
一扫千家愁绪。

注：

麻溪铺，在沅江南岸，城区以西。

Tune: Dreamlike Song

—Maxipu, Yuanling, 1949

East wind leaves no remnant snow lain,

In April every village is dying for rain,

Every heart burns in pain.

Suddenly clouds on hill's top gain,

Oh rain!

Oh rain!

Cleansing a thousand households' pain.

Note:

Maxipu is to the south of Yuanjiang River, west of the downtown area.

浣溪沙
重游沅陵桃溪坪,1949

风送晚霞山外山,
桃溪源首有无间,
道边空屋剩危栏。

当日居民何处去?
如今留下水湾湾,
板桥斜跨白沙滩。

注:

桃溪坪,位于酉水左岸。抗日战争期间,由沅陵城区去白田头雅礼中学初中部,必经桃溪坪。当时,村中不少房屋租给从沦陷区逃难到这里的居民居住,今已人去屋空。

Tune: Silk-washing Stream

—Revisiting Taoxiping in Yuanling, 1949

Wind sends off evening glow mountain beyond mountain,

Half hidden and half visible is Taoxi's fountain,

Houses on the roadside are empty, with rails worm-eaten.

Former residents, where are they now?

The stream winds its way, alone and forsaken,

The board bridge spans the white bay, sorrow-laden.

Note:

Taoxiping is located to the left of Youshui River. In the wartime period, it was the only way from Yuanling to Yali Middle School (Junior High School Section) in Baitiantou. At the time, many villagers rented their houses to refugees from the enemy-occupied area. The houses are empty now.

七　绝
湖南泸溪，1949

日丽风和集市开，
乡间少女赶场来，
笑声几处因何起，
花布缝裙巧手裁。

注：

泸溪是苗族聚居的一个县城。

A Seven-character Quatrain

—Luxi, Hunan, 1949

A sunny and breezy day hails the fair,

Country girls gather for the jolly affair.

How come laughters here and there?

Cloth made into dresses by a hand rare.

Note:

Luxi is a county inhabited by the Miao ethnic group.

南歌子
山溪,1950

飞沫银花屑,
寒光白刃锋,
劈开峻岭几多重,
万里云天尽在碧波中。

岁月无穷日,
清流自向东,
春来借得一帆风,
四海三江何处不相通?

注:
这是作者20岁生日时填的一首词,以湘西的山溪为题,抒情言志。

Tune: A Southern Song

—Mountain streams, 1950

Froth splashes into silver scraps,

The edged peak glistens in chilling light,

How many ridges has cleaved its might?

The sky infinite on high in waters emerald loses its height.

Time goes on in perpetuality,

Clear stream flows eastward in its own right,

Setting sail on a breezy day in spring bright,

How cometh the four seas and three rivers do not unite?

Note:

This *ci*-lyric was composed by the author on his 20th birthday, in which he describes the mountain streams in western Hunan to speak of his aspiration.

钗头凤
湘西,山行,1951

林间绕,泥泞道,
深山雨后斜阳照。
溪流满,竹桥短,
岭横雾隔,
岁寒春晚,
返?返?返?

青青草,樱桃小,
渐行渐觉风光好。
云烟散,峰回转,
菜花十里,
一川平坦,
赶!赶!赶!

注:
这是作者以山行为题,既写景,又抒陈个人抱负的一首词。

Tune: Phoenix Hairpin

—A mountain trip in western Hunan, 1951

The land woody, the road muddy,

The sun slanted on the rain-showered mountain moisty.

Full was the creek, short the bamboo plank,

Ridges blocked my way, fog my view blurred,

The weather was cold, spring slack—

Back, back, back?

Grass greeny, cherries tiny,

As I walked slowly, the landscape unrolled slowly.

Mist sank, the peak changed its track,

Ten-mile rape flowers straight,

A smooth stretch without break—

Quick, quick, quick!

Note:

This poem takes a mountain trip as the theme. Between the depiction of the landscape is the author's ambition at heart.

南乡子
湖南益阳渡口,1951

路北旧祠堂,

杂草枯藤断裂墙,

祖辈风光流水去,

沧桑,

前代空为后代忙。

道口树成行,

阵阵飘来果味香,

甜杏稍黄还带绿,

装筐,

三日航程到岳阳。

注:

作者由湖南沅陵到长沙参加高考,途经益阳。当时没有资江大桥,长途汽车在益阳渡口排队上船,摆渡过江。

Tune: Song of a Southern Country

—At the ferry in Yiyang, Hunan, 1951

On the road's north stands an old ancestral temple,

With grass rank, vines withered, and walls likely to topple.

Past glories went away with running water,

Everything shifts,

Old generation strived for the young, fruitless and futile.

Along the causeway trees lie in a row,

Gusts of wind the scent of mellow fruits blow.

Sweet apricots are yellow-green in color,

Into baskets,

Yueyang-bound, they have three days to go.

Note:

The author left Yuanling for Changsha, Hunan to take the National College Entrance Examination, by way of Yiyang. As Zijiang Bridge was not in existence then, long-distance buses had to queue at the ferry in Yiyang to be ferried across the river.

诉衷情

在长沙接到北京大学录取通知书有感，1951

几回翘首盼佳音，
喜报值千金。
拆函双手微抖，
好讯终来临。

如拂晓，
闯深林，
莫分心。
四年攻读，
错失良机，
有路难寻。

注：

通知书上载明，限九月初去北京大学报到。

A Confession

—Receiving Peking University Letter of Admission in Changsha, 1951

Many a time on tiptoe I pined for news good,
A happy message worth a thousand gold.
Hands trembled to open the letter,
At last the expected tidings to unfold!

Like going into woods deep,
When earth wakes from its sleep,
A heart undivided we keep.
The study four years to last,
Allows no opportunity to be missed,
Lest you get lost on your trip.

Note:

It was required in the letter that Li should report for duty in early September.

菩萨蛮
别长沙，1951

平堤沙岸湘江渡，
娇红艳紫湘山树。
湘水自多情，
欢腾送我行。

无穷留恋意，
伴逐霞云起。
何处不逢春，
春光不待人。

注：

作者于1951年8月下旬接到北京大学经济系录取通知书，随即乘火车由长沙到北京。

Tune: Buddha-like Dancers

—Farewell to Changsha, 1951

Flat dyke and sandy bank lie along the Xiangjiang River,

Trees bloom in red and purple on Xiang mountains all over.

Tender is Xiang water's nature,

Billowing all the way along my departure.

Immense is my reluctance to go,

Rising with clouds in glow.

Spring lands on every mile,

But for no man it tarries a while.

Note:

Upon receiving the Letter of Admission to the Department of Economics of Peking University in the latter part of August, 1951, the author left Changsha for Beijing by train right away.

柳梢青
北京大学沙滩校园白楼法学院图书馆，1951

学海无边，

好书自选，

哪顾休闲？

如此清幽，

一人静读，

窗外秋天。

夜深思索难眠，

念今古，才俊万千。

各有专攻，

浅尝止步，

悔恨年年。

注：

1951年新学年开始，除新生外，文科高年级（二、三、四年级和研究生）和绝大部分文科教师都到广西参加土改去了。因此，法学院图书馆内只有极少数人在看书。

Tune: Green Willow Twigs

—Written at the Law School Library in the White Building of Peking University, Shatan Section, 1951

The sea of study is boundless,

Good books free in abundance,

Whence the time for idleness?

In tranquility divine as such,

Quietly and alone I read, when

Autumn fills the blue vastness.

Thought bound, night finds me sleepless,

Then and now, plenty are men of excellence.

Each has his own specialty,

But with a smattering cut short early,

Falling prey to regrets endless.

Note:

Beginning from the new semester of 1951, with the exception of freshmen, senior students (sophomores, third and fourth grades and graduate students) as well as most teachers in the literary sciences went to Guangxi on account of the land reform movement. As a result, only a few students were studying at the Law School Library.

卜算子

冬至日，偕赵辉杰、马雍
散步从沙滩到安定门外，1951

盼到雪停时，
落叶埋尘土，
步出城门缓缓行，
谈笑河边路。

旧友与新知，
共赏冬青树。
偶见寒天北雁来，
飞过无寻处。

注：
旧友指赵辉杰，新知指刚结识的马雍。

Tune: Song of Divination

—On Winter Solstice Day, walking with Zhao Huijie and Ma Yong from Shatan to Andingmenwai, 1951

When snow stopped in time due,

And dust fallen leaves covered,

Slowly walked we out of the city gate,

Talking and laughing along the riverside.

Friend old and acquaintance new,

Together the evergreens we admired.

Haply a wild goose flew across the sky cold,

Leaving no trace in its glide.

Note:

Old friend refers to Zhao Huijie, and new acquaintance is Ma Yong.

减字木兰花
北河沿,春节,1952

春来缓缓,
南下雁群归去晚。
春在邻家,
小院墙头一树花。

春情渺渺,
断断续续河畔草。
春又无踪,
昨夜风沙枝上空。

注:

作者大学一年级时住在北京城内北河沿北京大学宿舍,寒假在北京度过。这是作者在北京经历的第一个寒冬。

Tune: Magnolia in Shortened Form

—Beiheyan, Spring Festival, 1952

Spring comes slow,

Wild geese on their return journey reluctant to go.

Spring calls on next door,

A tree of flowers beyond the yard's wall.

Spring becomes vague,

Grasses along the riverside drag.

Spring is no more,

Last night's sandy wind swept all that boughs bore.

Note:

When he was a freshman, the author lived in Peking University's dormitory in Beiheyan and spent his winter vacation in Beijing. It was the first winter he spent in Beijing.

西江月
路过海淀冰窖胡同,1952

今日平民混住,
当年内府群工。
冰砖堆砌窖藏中,
只为皇家享用。

世道而今变换,
平湖依旧冰封。
有谁水下顶寒风,
切割方形运送?

注:

西郊北京大学南门外向东不远,路南有一冰窖胡同。据说清朝时,派专人冬季在颐和园昆明湖上切割冰块,窖藏于冰窖胡同地下,夏季再运往皇宫,供消暑用。

Tune: The Moon over the West River

—Passing Bingjiao Hutong in Haidian district, 1952

A hotchpotch for civilians today,

Cabinet craftsmen convened hither.

Ice blocks were piled up in the cellar,

Exclusively to serve royal pleasure.

The world has changed now,

Though the lake is frozen as ever.

Do men still brave the cold in water,

To cut blocks icy and carry them away in summer?

Note:

Bingjiao Hutong lies not far from the south gate of Peking University in the western suburb to the east. It is said that in the Qing dynasty, people were asked to cut ice blocks on Kunming Lake in the Summer Palace on winter days, and stored them away underneath Bingjiao Hutong to be carried to the Imperial Palace in summer to relieve summer heat.

桃源忆故人
北京大学迁到西郊后遇见中学同学姚子范,1952

免遭战火湘西住,
有幸同窗相处。
一别数年未晤,
犹记沅江渡。

燕园遍地丁香树,
春到莺飞蝶舞。
莫让时光辜负,
留梦京郊路。

注:

姚子范,湖南醴陵人,长作者一岁,1950年考取清华大学经济系。1952年院系调整,清华大学经济系并入北京大学经济系。

Thinking of an Old Friend in Taoyuan

—Meeting my middle-school fellow Yao Zifan after Peking University moved to the western suburb, 1952

In western Hunan we lived, warfare to avoid,

Lucky to have you by my side.

For years departed and unmet,

The memory of Yuanjiang sticks in my mind.

Lilac trees spread all over the Yan Garden wide,

Where warblers fly and butterflies dance in spring tide.

Do not idle away and bide,

Leaving dreams unfulfilled on the countryside.

Note:

Yao Zifan, a native of Liling, Hunan province, is a year older than Li. He was admitted to the Economic Department of Tsinghua University in 1950. When the departments and schools were adjusted in 1952, the Economic Department of Tsinghua University was merged into the Economic Department of Peking University.

采桑子
颐和园，1953

佛香阁上看湖小，
只道山高。
谁道山高，
见否群峰水底漂？

半池荷叶遮行路，
懒把舟摇。
待把舟摇，
别有风光玉带桥。

注：
这是一首以颐和园风景为题的自勉之作。

Tune: Picking Mulberries

—The Summer Palace, 1953

Looking from the Buddhist Pavilion the lake is small,

The hill is tall.

Who deems the hills tall?

See in its floor water embrace them all?

Lotus leaves block half of the pond,

Idly I would not roll the oar.

When I roll the oar.

The Jade Belt Bridge in its best comes to the fore.

Note:

This is a self-encouraging poem with the Summer Palace as its topic.

十六字令
无题,1954

书,
尽信前人难自如。
勤思索,
掩卷费踟蹰。

注:
图书馆归来。

A Sixteen-word Song

—No title, 1954

Books,

Believe them all, you can't stand tall.

Sharpen your brain,

Hesitate before swallowing them all.

Note:

This poem was written after the author returned from the library.

减字木兰花
陪赵迺抟老师、骆涵素师母游香山,1955

繁华浅草,

蜂蝶随人花径小。

云淡风清,

春色依然岭上明。

山高几许,

手插柳条逢喜雨。

幼树新姿,

共盼迎来飞絮时。

注:

赵迺抟老师,北京大学经济系教授。师母骆涵素教授,任教于北京师范大学。

Tune: Magnolia in Shortened Form

—Touring Fragrant Hills with my teacher Zhao Naituan and his wife Luo Hansu, 1955

Flowers luxuriant, grasses shallow,
Bees and butterflies flutter along flowery lanes narrow.
The cloud light, the wind fresh,
The mountain has the best of spring to relish.

High is the hill,
Willow twigs in hand, rain falls to our will.
Small trees in new stance,
Together we wait to see catkins in the air dance.

Note:

Zhao Naituan was a professor in the Economic Department of Peking University. Professor Luo Hansu, his wife, taught at Beijing Normal University.

鹧鸪天
大学毕业自勉，1955

溪水清清下石沟，
千弯百折不回头，
兼容并蓄终宽阔，
若谷虚怀鱼自游。

心寂寂，念休休，
沉沙无意却成洲，
一生治学当如此，
只计耕耘莫问收。

注：
作者1955年毕业于北京大学经济系，留校工作至今。

Tune: Partridge Sky

—A self-encouraging poem written upon university graduation, 1955

Down the ditch flows the stream clean and clear,

Twisting and turning without a look in the rear,

Her size expands along her journey all-inclusive,

Her bosom opens for fishes to swim free of fear.

Heart in peace, mind without care,

Sands form into an islet unaware—

A model for lifetime scholarly research to follow:

Do what you can, but never ask how you fare.

Note:

After graduating from the Economic Department of Peking University in 1955, Li has worked at the university until now.

七　绝
重读周邦彦词，1956

风老莺雏梅子黄，
春归无影忆渔郎。
隋堤折柳送行客，
词在精工不在狂。

注：

周邦彦，北宋词人，精通音律，曾任管理乐府的官员。他的词精雕细刻，自成一家。

A Seven-character Quatrain

—Rereading the *ci*-lyrics of Zhou Bangyan, 1956

Chicks grow in the wind, plums turn yellow,

Spring unseen, memories of the young fisherman come slow.

Willow twigs on the Sui Dyke bid friends farewell,

The essence of *ci* lies in refinement than wild bellow.

Note:

Zhou Bangyan was a Northern-Song-dynasty poet and Yuefu officer renowned for his mastery of rhythms. His *ci*-lyrics were precise and refined in a manner of his own.

浣溪沙
为何玉春题照，1957

谁解春游少女心，
迷人黄蝶最知音，
翩翩引路小河滨。

先摘蔷薇红辫结，
再临流水整纱巾，
笑声惊散细鱼群。

注：

这首词试用拼音韵。

Tune: Silk-washing Stream

—Written for He Yuchun's photo, 1957

Who can read a lady's mind in her spring tour?
Most intimate is the yellow butterfly for sure,
Fluttering its way towards a small stream pure.

A rose to tie on her braid for a start,
Then her scarf rearranged by the flowing water,
Her smile scatters schools of tiny fish asunder.

Note:

This lyric poem was a trial on Pinyin rhyme.

五　绝
无题，1957

花间立誓词，
贵在两心知，
此意何须改，
白头回忆时。

注：

定情之作。

A Five-character Quatrain

—No title, 1957

Pledged we among the flowers,

Precious are two linked hearts of ours.

Wherefore the change of mind?

Grey-haired we recall past hours.

Note:

This poem was written as a pledge of love.

浣溪沙
除夕,1958

静院深庭小雪霏,
炉边相聚说春归,
窗灯掩映辫儿垂。

笑忆初逢询玉镜,
含羞不语指红梅,
劝尝甜酒换银杯。

注:

1958年2月,农历除夕,作者与何玉春结婚。"玉镜"一词引自东晋温峤故事,后来被用作"聘礼"的代词。

Tune: Silk-washing Stream

—On Lunar New Year's Eve, 1958

Snow drifted about in the quiet yard hidden deep,
Around the stove chatted we over spring's back trip,
Your braid drooped long against the window lamp.

Merrily we recalled the "jade mirror" on our first date,
You pointed to the red plum, silence demure to keep,
Persuading me sweet wine to drink for the silver cup.

Note:

The couple married on Lunar New Year's Eve in February 1958. "Jade mirror" is quoted from the story about Wen Qiao in the Eastern Jin dynasty, as a substitute for "bride-price".

人月圆
题结婚照，1958

辛勤手织毛衣绿，
今日代婚纱。
素妆淡抹，
胸前点缀，
一朵红花。

平房砖地，
小窗剪纸，
装扮新家。
明晨离去，
银河无路，
地角天涯。

注：

作者在婚前已将外祖母、母亲与弟弟以平从武汉接到北京来住，在海淀苏公家庙4号租了三小间简陋的平房，合在一起不过20平方米。

Tune: The Full Moon

—A poem for our wedding photo, 1958

Green sweater knitted by hands untiring,
Your wedding dress made in disguise.
Make-up simple and light,
On your chest,
A red flower glows.

The bungalow brick-floored,
With windows paper-cuts adorned,
Became the new home of ours.
The next morning saw our parting,
The milk way barred our meeting,
You and I asunder in pining hours.

Note:

Before marriage the author had already brought his grandmother, mother and brother from Wuhan to live with him in Beijing. He rented three small bungalows at No. 4, Sugongjiamiao, Haidian, altogether 20 square meters only.

天仙子
送赵辉杰赴兰州,1958

把手送君西北去,
莫问边城晴或雨,
祁连山下过春风,
休犹豫,
请记取,
塞上也能飘柳絮。

人世悠悠长几许,
往事只当初写序,
黄河润笔著新篇,
惊人语,
千万句,
留待他年杯酒叙。

注:

赵辉杰,作者在湖南雅礼中学同学,1958年自北京大学史学系研究生毕业,分配到兰州大学任教。

Tune: Song of Immortals

—Seeing Zhao Huijie Off to Lanzhou, 1958

Hands shaking, I send you northwest yonder,

Never mind rain or sun on the border.

When spring blows across Qilian Mountain,

Hesitate never,

But remember,

Catkins will as well fly on the frontier.

Long is our journey on the human world hither,

Past events but a preface to a new chapter.

Write with a pen drenched in the Yellow River,

Many a thriller,

Large in number,

Reserve them for talks over wine years later.

Note:

Zhao Huijie was a schoolmate of Li Yining during his study at Yali Middle School. After finishing his master's degree in history at Peking University in 1958, Zhao was allotted to Lanzhou University as a teacher.

踏莎行
斋堂，修渠，1958

截水移流，
开山筑坝，
云梯铁索空中架，
百花山侧走蛟龙，
遥看龙首飞泉下。

一脉龙身，
双峰桥跨，
悠悠龙尾几分岔？
三支清水绕村流，
无边秀色谁能画？

注：

斋堂位于北京市门头沟区，是穷困山区。1958年春节前到1959年春节前，北京大学部分教职员下放门头沟区。作者与经济系、法律系、生物系教职员一起被分配到斋堂乡西斋堂村劳动一年。

Tune: Treading on Grass

—Repairing a ditch at Zhaitang, 1958

Cut the water, change its flow,

Open the mountain, build a dam,

Hang a ladder iron-chained in the mighty dome.

Along the floral range the flood dragon wriggles,

Looked afar, its head plunges into the spring's realm.

Its majestic body long,

Twin peaks spans to fame.

Far-flung is its tail, how many are branches under its name?

Around the village three streams flow,

Who can replicate the beauty to the brim?

Note:

Situated in Mentougou district, Zhaitang was a poverty-stricken mountainous region in Beijing. From the period before the 1958 Spring Festival to the period before the 1959 Spring Festival, some faculty members of Peking University were transferred to Mentougou for manual labor. Li was allotted to Zhaitang village to the west of Zhaitang together with faculty members in the economic, law and biology departments for one year's labor.

采桑子
灵山脚下,夜宿农家,1958

山间小路花无语,
崖上青藤,
地上虫声,
多谢浮云送一程。

夜来风紧秋离去,
一盏油灯,
积雪几层?
错把三更作五更。

注:
灵山是北京市最高峰,位于门头沟区,海拔2300米。

Tune: Picking Mulberries

—Sleeping in a farmer's house under the foot of Lingshan Mountain, 1958

On the country road wild flowers bloom quiet,

Ivies crawl the cliff up,

Insects on the ground chirp,

So kind are floating winds escorting my trip.

Tight wind hastens away autumn overnight,

By the oil lamp,

How many layers is the snow deep?

I mistake the third watch for fifth in my sleep.

Note:

Situated in Mentougou district, the 2300-meter-high Lingshan Mountain is the highest peak in Beijing.

浣溪沙
无题,1959

燕子多情绕故城,
杨花飞尽了无声,
夜阑人静听残更。

又是池塘春水绿,
几回天外鹊桥横,
半庭青草为谁生?

注:

婚后两地分居,以词表达思念之情。

Tune: Silk-washing Stream

—No title, 1959

Over the old town swallows affectionately hover,

Poplar catkins in silence fly into thin air,

In the dead of night I am a lonely listener.

Once more the pool is emerald with spring water,

How many times did the magpie bridge spanned yonder,

For whom the green grass grows, half of the yard over?

Note:

The author and his wife lived apart after marriage. This poem was written to express his lovesickness.

鹊桥仙
三十岁生日,独自骑车游圆明园遗址,1960

半池衰草,

几经风雨,

只剩几株野菊。

西风过后又初霜,

照旧是花黄叶绿。

茫茫人世,

漫长苦旅,

一生如同弈局。

荣枯顺逆俱寻常,

总难免弯弯曲曲。

注:

当时的圆明园遗址残破萧索,几乎没有什么游人。

Tune: Immortals on the Magpie Bridge

—Written upon my 30th birthday, riding alone to Yuanmingyuan Park, 1960

Half a pool of withered plants,

After rounds of autumn rain,

A few wild chrysanthemums remain.

When the west wind goes frost comes as usual,

Flowers are yellow, leaves green again.

Vast is this earthly world,

Long the journey in pain,

Life is a game of chess to lose or gain.

Prosperity and adversity are both normal,

Twists and turns no one can detain.

Note:

Yuanmingyuan Park at the time was a scene of desolation, with few tourists.

南乡子
记厉放患麻疹并发肺炎,何玉春连夜自鞍山赶回北京,1962

急电促回京,
仆仆风尘两地行,
未进家门先缓步,
轻轻,
小女今宵怕受惊。

淡月照中庭,
最贵人间母子行,
彻夜披衣床角坐,
天明,
再测高烧可退清。

注:

厉放此时三岁半。

Tune: Song of a Southern Country

—Lines composed to mark He Yuchun's coming to Beijing from Anshan the very night when Li Fang was down with measles and pneumonia, 1962

An urgent call from the capital,
Off she went, hasty and weary withal.
At the doorstep her steps slowed,
Gentle,
Not to frighten her lass little.

The moon shone on the yard behind its veil,
Most precious in the world is love maternal.
By the bedside she stayed up, coat on shoulder,
Till morning's signal,
To check if the temperature has returned normal.

Note:

Li Fang, the author's daughter, was three and a half years old at the time.

浣溪沙
无题,1962

几见西风送晚霞,
小园开遍一年花,
篱边人去影留家。

眼底离愁谁似我,
银宫寂寞不如她,
飞尘又满绿窗纱。

注:
相思之苦,全在词中。

Tune: Silk-washing Stream

—No title, 1962

Many a time the zephyr sends away sunset glow,

All year round flowers keep the yard aglow,

By the hedge she left, but not so her shadow.

The deepest sorrow is on me without peer,

In her lonely bower sits she in saddest woe,

Dust re-covers my green window screen, lo!

Note:

The author's lovesickness is fully expressed in this *ci*-lyric.

鹧鸪天
中秋,1963

一纸家书两地思,
忍看明月照秋池,
邻家夫妇团圆夜,
正是门前盼信迟。

情脉脉,意丝丝,
试将心事付新词,
几回搁笔难成曲,
纵使曲成只自知。

注:
中秋月明,倍添思念之情,遂有此作。

Tune: Partridge Sky

—Middle Autumn, 1963

A letter from home, two longing hearts blue,

The bright moon upon the autumn pool was a doleful view,

Neighbors enjoyed their connubial reunion,

Night found me alone at doorstep, waiting for letters overdue.

Tender is my love, soft my sentiment true,

My thoughts I tried to convey to lines new,

But oft gave it up, failing to compose a tune,

Even if it was already in my mind, only I knew.

Note:

The moon at the Mid-Autumn Festival was so bright as to aggravate the author's lovesickness. Hence this poem.

七　绝

咏梅（窗前一株梅树，与我作伴已数年），1964

朝朝相伴谁人栽？
有意有情独自开，
花落花飞浑不觉，
只知窗下暗香来。

注：

这时作者仍住在北京海淀区苏公家庙4号，夫妇两地分居已六年有余。

A Seven-character Quatrain

—To the old plum tree in front of my window, 1964

Who planted you, day after day standing where I dwell?

Feelingly and fondly bloom you, no one to tell.

Flowers fall and flowers fly, to my blind eye,

But below my window delicate fragrance I smell.

Note:

At the time the author still lived at No. 4, Sugongjiamiao, Haidian. It had been six years and more since the couple lived apart.

调笑令
记厉伟学步，1964

穿户，

穿户，

小燕巢边寻路。

轻轻两翼低挥，

停停又复起飞。

飞起，

飞起，

明日长空万里。

注：

厉伟，作者之子，生于1963年11月。

Tune: Song of Flirtation

—A poem for Li Wei learning to walk, 1964

Over the door,

Over the door,

A swallowling in nest tries to soar.

Gently it raises its wings low,

Stops, flies, once more to go.

Fly,

Fly,

Tomorrow in the broad sky you will soar high.

Note:

Li Wei, the author's son, was born in November 1963.

浪淘沙
船过湖北嘉鱼赤壁,1964

日出大江东,
碧野晴空,
白帆有意恋微风,
遥想当年鏖战夜,
感慨无穷。

开国赖军功,
父辈英雄,
子孙未必识弯弓,
司马根除曹魏日,
不见兵戎。

注:

曹魏晚期,大权落入司马昭之手。公元265年,曹魏末代皇帝曹奂被迫将皇位让给司马昭之子司马炎,魏亡晋立,此时距赤壁之战(208年)仅57年。

Tune: Sand-sifting Waves

—Passing Red Cliff in the county of Jiayu in Hubei by boat, 1964

The sun rises in the east of the Great River,
Green grass lies beneath the sky azure,
The white sail will not let go of the zephyr.
Thinking of the warring night bygone,
Emotions swell in me altogether.

The founding of a nation depends on military endeavor,
Full many a heroic forefather,
Their posterities may not know a bow's maneuver.
When Sima defeated the state of Wei,
Weapons did not appear.

Note:

In its late period, the state of Wei lost its power to Sima Zhao. In AD 265, Cao Huan, the last emperor of the state of Wei, was forced to abdicate his reign to Sima Yan, son of Sima Zhao. By that abdication, the state of Wei was succeeded by the state of Jin. It was only 57 years since the War of Red Cliff in AD 208.

南乡子
湖北江陵城外所见,1964

荒野一空楼,

独照枯枝月正愁。

满院萧条人早去,

啾啾,

只剩虫声日夜留。

处世似行舟,

听任东西缓缓流。

荆楚繁华终是梦,

幽幽,

江上渔歌好个秋。

注:

江陵,楚国都城,南朝时后梁亦建都于此。唐朝以后一直是商业城市。清末起,逐渐衰败。

Tune: Song of a Southern Country

—Outside the city of Jiangling, Hubei, 1964

An empty tower looms in the wilderness,

The moon shines on withered boughs in woeful loneliness.

People long gone, the yard is a scene of dilapidation,

Chirp, chirp,

Only the sound of insects persists in light and darkness.

Life in this world is like a boat's race,

East or west, follow the water at a slow pace.

Prosperity in the state of Chu is but a dream,

Hush, hush,

Fishing songs upon the river make autumn so nice.

Note:

Jiangling was the capital of the state of Chu. The Later Liang dynasty also established its capital there. Since the Tang dynasty Jiangling had remained a commercial city until the late Qing dynasty when it began to decline.

朝中措
湖北江陵滩桥,春节,1965

江村一夜换新容,

户户对联红。

巧妇赶熏鱼肉,

顽儿笑舞灯笼。

农家作客,

炭盆围坐,

米酒浓浓。

习俗城乡虽异,

人情南北皆同。

注:

滩桥是江陵县的一个区。当时作者和北京大学经济系师生分散住在滩桥人民公社各个大队。

Tune: Measures at Court

—At Tanqiao in Jiangling, Hubei in the 1965 Spring Festival, 1965

The riverside village put on a new look overnight,

Every door with red couplets was a bright sight.

Handy women were busy making smoked meat and fish,

Naughty children played with lanterns in delight.

Guests came to a farmer's house,

Around a brazier of charcoal they sat,

The rice wine smelt alright.

Customs differed in cities and towns,

North and south the same sentiment possessed.

Note:

Tanqiao is a district in Jiangling county. At the time Li and other teachers and students of the Economic Department of Peking University lived among different groups of the People's Commune in Tanqiao.

柳梢青
带厉放、厉伟散步到北京海淀六郎庄，1965

稻叶青青，

莲花几朵，

浅沼浮萍。

一湾流水，

小桥杨柳，

斜挂稀星。

暮云变幻无形，

纵凉意，难卜雨晴。

变幻由他，

且看儿女，

捕捉蜻蜓。

注：

六郎庄位于北京大学西南门外约两公里处。

Tune: Green Willow Twigs

—Walking with Li Fang and Li Wei to Liulangzhuang in Haidian district, 1965

Green rice leaves,

Several lotus flowers,

A pond of weeds afloat.

Flowing water in a strip,

Willows beside a small bridge,

Sparse stars on a slant.

Evening clouds change fast,

Rain or shine, coldness neither can predict.

Change as it may,

I will watch my son and daughter,

Chasing butterflies in delight.

Note:

Liulangzhuang is about two kilometers to the southwest gate of Peking University.

忆秦娥
北京建国门桥头，1965

梅开后，

河桥景色还依旧，

还依旧。

漫天飞雪，

寒衣凉透。

当时谁料分离久，

怎知别梦年年有，

年年有。

那边瞭望，

华灯如昼。

注：

1965年冬，作者在北京朝阳区农村，送何玉春回辽宁鞍山工作。距发车还有一段时间，偕何玉春步行至建国门桥头。何玉春上车后，作者深夜冒雪骑自行车回到20公里外的乡间。此情此景，一生难忘。

Tune: Thinking of a Qin Lady

—On Jianguomen Bridge, Beijing, 1965

The plums come into flower,

The view over the bridge remains as ever,

As ever.

In the sky snowflakes whirl,

Thoroughly cold am I in my winter apparel.

Who could have expected such a long departure?

Accompanied by dreams of departing year after year,

Year after year.

Light bright as day,

There yonder.

Note:

In the winter of 1965, when he lived at a village in Chaoyang district, Li sent his wife back to work in Anshan, Liaoning. Before the train set off, they walked to Jianguomen Bridge. Seeing her train gone, Li rode over twenty kilometers back to his abode in the snowy night. That experience will remain in his heart for a lifetime.

破阵子
昌平北太平庄，1968

乱石堆前野草，
雄关影里荒滩。
千嶂沉云昏白日，
百里狂沙隐碧山，
此心依旧丹。

隔世浑然容易，
忘情我却为难。
既是三江春汛到，
不信孤村独自寒，
花开转瞬间。

注：
这首词写于昌平北太平庄"监改大院"内。

Tune: Dance of the Calvary

—Beitaipingzhuang, Changping, 1968

Grasses ran riot before a pile of stones,

Strong Pass loomed large on a land of wilderness.

The sun blurred in a thousand layers of low clouds,

Green hills dimmed in a hundred miles of sand coarse,

A loyal heart kept I in consistence.

To endure separation in space is easy,

To be indifferent is beyond my competence.

Now that fishing season has come to the Three Rivers,

No village will be left alone in coldness,

Flowers bloom in a trice.

Note:

This *ci*-lyric was written in "the yard of inspection and reform" in Beitaipingzhuang, Changping.

昭君怨

去江西途中,车过杭州,天已黑,先雨后晴,一夜难眠,1969

晴日落尘处处,
微雨有缘洗树。
梦中也思家,
满园花。

久闯江湖渐老,
又见枯枝衰草。
窗外北风狂,
月昏黄。

注:

刚离开北京,车内无人不思家。

Tune: Zhaojun's Complain

—Passing Hangzhou on my Jiangxi-bound journey, a sleepless night after rain, 1969

On sunny days dust falls everywhere,

A timely shower cleans trees fair.

My home haunts me, even in dreams,

With its yard of flowers.

Old am I after years' strife in this earthly tour,

To find grass dead and boughs bare.

Outside the north wind rages,

The moon blurs.

Note:

All people in the train were homesick then.

七 绝
在鲤鱼洲度过39岁生日,1969

恍然一梦醒何迟,
惊觉已临不惑时,
风送落花飞似雪,
来年春在小桃枝。

注:
1969年10月下旬到达江西南昌鲤鱼洲,一个月后就是作者39岁生日。

A Seven-character Quatrain

—Spending my 39th birthday in Liyuzhou, 1969

I dreamed a dream and woke up late,

Alarmed to find myself upon forty's gate.

Wind sent flowers flying like snow, next year

Spring will on a tiny peach bough wait.

Note:

The author arrived at Liyuzhou, Nanchang in Jiangxi province in the latter half of October 1969, one month before his 39th birthday.

七 古
鲤鱼洲上所见，1970

荒村春夜人皆睡，
忽见堤坡有影来。
衣衫破旧不遮体，
扶老携妻带幼孩。
自称家舍在市外，
山地无雨已成灾，
逃荒只为保残命，
母病儿小饥难挨。
但求两碗热面糊，
草草喝完再赶路。
原来还有更穷人，
今日深知百姓苦。

注：

在鲤鱼洲上，经常看到前来讨饭的灾民。

A Seven-character Rhymed Poem

—What I saw in Liyuzhou, 1970

On a spring night in the deserted village fast asleep,

A shadow suddenly came into sight on the mound.

His shabby clothes barely covered his body,

His mother, wife and child trailed behind.

He said his home was outside the city, where

Drought had caused a disaster to his land.

They fled and begged to keep their humble living,

For ill was his mother, and his child in dire want of food.

Two bowls of hot paste they asked for,

Which they finished off to continue their journey.

Alas! Poor I am, but there should be people more than poor!

The hardship of common people as such sinks deep in me.

Note:

In Liyuzhou, one can often see refugees begging for food.

浣溪沙
中秋节，于鲤鱼洲，1970

巍巍庐山枕碧流，

时光飞驰过中秋，

风摇芦苇自飕飕。

日落西堤牛进舍，

云开东岸数归舟，

争看明月照荒洲。

注：

军宣队从北京运来月饼，每人发两块。月饼名"自来红"，很硬，但大家都吃了。

Tune: Silk-washing Stream

—Mid-Autumn in Liyuzhou, 1970

Lofty Lushan pillows on emerald flow,

Time fleets to the Mid-Autumn like an arrow,

Reeds sway when wind whistles its blow.

By the sun westward the lowing herd return home,

As eastern clouds dispel we count boats back in a row,

Jostling to look at the moon beaming on the bleak mass below.

Note:

The military propaganda team brought mooncakes from Beijing, two for each.

"Zilaihong", as the mooncake was called, was very hard, but they ate them all.

相见欢
四十自述,1970

几经风雨悲欢,

志未残,

试探人间行路有何难。

时如箭,

心不变,

道犹宽,

莫待他年空叹鬓毛斑。

注:

作者生于1930年,40岁生日在鲤鱼洲上度过。

Tune: Meeting in Delight

—A self-account upon my 40th birthday, 1970

Winds and rains I have weathered through, happy or sad,

My will remain unchanged.

How come difficulties in life's journey on this land?

Time fleets like an arrow,

My heart unswerving as ever so.

Broad is the road,

Do not wait and sigh till grey haired.

Note:

The author spent his 40th birthday in Liyuzhou.

鹧鸪天
迎何玉春来鲤鱼洲,1971

往事难留一笑中,
离愁十载去无踪,
银锄共筑田边路,
茅屋同遮雨后风。

朝露冷,晚霞红,
门前夜夜稻香浓,
纵然汗渍斑斑在,
胜似关山隔万重。

注:
作者夫妇婚后13年一直两地分居,这时终于团聚了。

Tune: Partridge Sky

—Reuniting with He Yuchun in Liyuzhou, 1971

Past events irretrievable, I give it a smile,

Ten years' sorrow asunder vanishes without trail.

Silver hoes in hand, together we build roads along the field,

A thatch is enough to shelter us when rain and wind befall.

Cold is the dew, rosy the sunset glow,

Before our door sweet scents from the rice field blow.

Never minding sweats streaming down,

Most painful are forts and hills severing us years ago.

Note:

After 13 years' separation, the author reunited with his wife at last.

鹧鸪天
赠何玉春，鲤鱼洲，1971

堤外有堤洲上洲，
渡船撑出小河沟。
花开两岸红黄紫，
草绿平台春夏秋。

晴日暖，晚风柔，
江南斗笠好遮头。
今年学做庄稼事，
汗水权当雨水流。

注：

"花开两岸红黄紫"是鲤鱼洲春天一景。红色的，是当作绿肥的红花草；黄色的，是油菜花；紫色的，是蚕豆花。

Tune: Partridge Sky

—A poem for He Yuchun written in Liyuzhou, 1971

Dyke beyond dyke, isle upon isle,

The ferry boat steers out of the brook small.

Flowers flank the bank in red, yellow and purple,

Grass greens the platform in spring, summer and fall.

The sun shines warm, evening breeze blows gentle,

The hat in Jiangnan style protects my head well.

The art of plantation I learn this year,

Despite sweat trickling down my face like rainfall.

Note:

"Flowers flanked the bank in red, yellow and purple" is a unique scene in springtime Liyuzhou. "Red" are Chinese milk velch used as manure, "yellow" are rape flowers, and "purple" broadbean flowers.

七 律
四十五岁生日,于大兴县农村,1975

落泊京华已半生,

难求闭户读书声。

行舟从未风相助,

匹马偏逢路纵横。

愧叹吟诗非七步,

黯然练笔靠三更。

愿如厚积山头雪,

日暖消融溪自成。

注:

传说唐初诗人王勃乘船去江西探望父亲,因有神风相助,迅速舟抵南昌,遂有《滕王阁序》之作。"七步",相传三国魏曹植才思敏捷,七步成诗。

A Seven-character Regulated Verse

—Written upon my 45th birthday at a village in Daxing county, 1975

Half of my life I spent in Beijing, low and poor,
Failing to find reading time behind closed door.
Never did a wind come in favor of my boat,
On horseback roads crisscrossed before.
Alas! Unable to make a poem in seven steps,
I practiced hard in the depth of night withal.
May it like thick snows on tip of mountains,
When the days get warm, into streams they thaw.

Note:

It is said that Wang Bo, a famed poet in the early Tang dynasty, wrote his masterpiece "Prelude to Tengwang Pavilion" after a magic wind speeded his boat to Nanchang so that he could see his father in the earliest time. Another legend has it that Cao Zhi, the smart son of Cao Cao, wrote a poem within the time of seven steps.

采桑子
北京一月街景,1976

声声哀乐催人泪,

处处灵堂,

处处花墙,

一夜京城换素妆。

音容虽已天边去,

留下忧伤,

留下彷徨,

预感风来雨更狂。

注:

记述周恩来总理逝世时的情景。此时作者正在北京大兴县农村。

Tune: Picking Mulberries

—Beijing in January, a street scene, 1976

Dirges unending, tears nonstop,

Mourning halls everywhere,

Wreath walls everywhere,

Over a night the city changes to a plain wear.

Gone beyond the sky is his countenance,

Leaving desolation,

Leaving hesitation,

Foreboding rain abreast of gale in augmentation.

Note:

This is a description about Premier Zhou Enlai's death. At the time the author was at a village in Daxing county.

调笑令
送厉放到昌平马池口公社西坨村插队，1977

飞雪，

飞雪，

大地生机未绝。

且看三月春晴，

又是漫山草青。

青草，

青草，

雪后成长更俏。

注：

厉放赶上了高中毕业生下乡插队的"末班车"。

Tune: Song of Flirtation

—Sending Li Fang to work in Xituo village, Machikou Commune in Changping, 1977

Snow flies,

Snow flies,

Life on earth not dies.

Just wait till the sun shines in March serene,

When the hill again brims with grass green.

Green grass,

Green grass,

More divine it becomes after snow's caress.

Note:

Li Fang caught up with the "last bus" for high-school graduates to work in the country.

南歌子
元旦有感，1979

坡险人烟少，
沟深草木稀，
路标令我暗生疑，
遇阻绕行见否小山溪？

乐曲应重谱，
文章再破题，
有心攀上最高梯，
此去何方一览尽无疑。

注：

中共十一届三中全会刚结束，作者决心投入改革的探索与研究。

Tune: A Southern Song

—Lines composed on New Year's Day, 1979

On steep slopes people are scarce,

In deep ditches vegetation is few,

To me the road signs become a suspicious cue,

Obstacles passed round, are there small streams in view?

The music should be recomposed,

The subject be considered anew,

Mind set on the crest to subdue,

A glance mere gives the way ahead a clear clue.

Note:

After the Third Plenary Session of the 11th Central Committee of the Communist Party, Li was prepared to dedicate himself to the exploration and research of China's reform.

七　绝

由北京赴杭州，车过安徽凤阳，1979

淮上农家换笑颜，

曙光已在晓云边，

山川垅亩还依旧，

却见人人争下田。

注：

开始于安徽凤阳的农村承包制，正逐渐在全国推广。

A Seven-character Quatrain

—Journey from Beijing to Hangzhou, bypassing Fengyang in Anhui, 1979

Farmers in Huai switch to their smiling countenance,

Morning clouds already brighten in twilight radiance,

Mountains, rivers and ridged fields remain unchanged,

Curious to watch people go into the field in readiness.

Note:

The rural contract system started in Fengyang, Anhui gradually spread nationwide.

七 绝
无题，1980

隋代不循秦汉律，
明人不着宋人装，
陈规当变终须变，
留与儿孙评短长。

注：

1980年4-5月，作者参加了中共中央书记处研究室与国家劳动总局联合召开的劳动工资座谈会，讨论经济体制改革问题。这首诗是在会议期间写的。

A Seven-character Quatrain

—No title, 1980

Sui dynasty did not follow laws of Qin and Han,

Ming people would not keep Song's wardrobe.

Old rules should be discarded when need be,

Leave them for later generations to probe.

Note:

From April to May in 1980, the author attended a panel discussion on wage jointly sponsored by the Office of the Secretariat of the CPC Central Committee and State Bureau of Labor, on the issue about economic system reform. This poem was written during the meeting.

南乡子
五十岁生日,1980

往事忆难停,
留待他年细细评。
改革声中抒己见,
争鸣,
今后何须绕道行。

不再叹零丁,
多少名家聚北京。
迎接新潮成气势,
无形,
走向前方路渐明。

注:
讨论改革进程,已成为新风。

Tune: Song of a Southern Country

—Composed on my 50th birthday, 1980

Recollections of the past are endless,

Leave them to judgment for years to pass.

Expressing my view in the reforming wave, among Thoughts profuse,

There will be no need to detour along my course.

Sigh no more over loneliness,

Here in Beijing so many experts mass.

The acclaim for a new trend has gained momentum,

Shapeless,

The road ahead extends towards brightness.

Note:

The discussion about reform process has become a new trend.

鹧鸪天
游四川青城山有感，1981

洞穴深深好炼丹，
迢迢千里献高官。
贵人几个通灵性？
道在是非一念间。

登小阁，望前川，
缓流总比急流宽。
从来黄老天为治，
疏导顺情国自安。

注：

青城山，历代道士炼丹之处。词中"缓流总比急流宽"一句，充分表达了作者的经济思想。

Tune: Partridge Sky

—Touring Mount Qingchen in Sichuan, 1981

Deep is the cave, for magic pills a nice pick,

Long journey they travel, for dignitaries' sake.

But how many of them are spiritual-minded?

The Way lies in the idea of right and wrong in a wink.

Climbing the pavilion small, the river lies before,

Slow streams are always broader in form than streams quick.

The law of Heaven Huang-Lao school consistently observes,

Compliance with people's needs leads to social stability in sync.

Note:

Mount Qingcheng is a legendary Taoist site for alchemy. "Slow streams are always broader in form than streams quick" gives full expression to Li's economic thinking.

鹧鸪天
为厉伟考取北京大学化学系而作,1981

慈母夜深课子声,
春华秋实愿终成。
当初曾有理工志,
今日欣由汝继承。

墙上草,树间藤,
长年默默自攀升。
一生兴趣将多变,
知否前方路纵横?

注:

"当初曾有理工志"是指:作者1948年毕业于南京金陵中学高中部,因成绩优异,保送金陵大学,可自选专业、院系。作者选择的是化学工程系,但因后来参加工作,未去成。工作两年后,参加高考,被北京大学经济系录取。

Tune: Partridge Sky

—Composed upon Li Wei's admission to the Chemistry Department of Peking University, 1981

Mother's admonition the night went through,
Flowers bloomed, fruits bear, our wish comes true.
My ambition for technology keenly held yesterday,
A chance inheritance you happen to enjoy too.

Grass on the wall, vines between trees,
Quietly they climb upward, as they always do.
A man's interest will change through his life,
Crisscrosses lie in store as roads unroll before you.

Note:

"My ambition for technology keenly held yesterday": Upon graduation from Jinling Middle School in Nanjing in 1948, thanks to his excellent performance, Li was recommended to Jinling University for admission, major and department free to choose. Li chose chemical engineering, but already at work, he was unable to go in the end. When sitting for the National College Entrance Examination after two years' work, he was admitted to the Department of Economics of Peking University.

南歌子
游漓江,1982

昨夜逢春雨,
今朝雾满江,
奇峰俏丽似新娘,
半隐半明带羞着纱装。

含蓄人间美,
自然意味长。
吟诗作画亦相当,
妙在容君日后慢思量。

注:
1982年春,作者夫妇应广西师范大学邀请,到桂林讲学。在学生罗知颂陪同下,雨中游漓江。

Tune: A Southern Song

—Touring Lijiang River, 1982

A spring shower last night,

A fog-drenched river this morning,

Strange peaks like a bride charming,

Half hidden, half seen, all coyness behind her veiling.

Implicit is Earth's beauty,

Deep Nature's meaning,

Poems and paintings are both befitting,

The wonder lies in subtle considerations in years coming.

Note:

In the spring of 1982, the couple went to Guilin for a scholarly purpose upon Guangxi Normal University's invitation, during which they made this tour in rain in the company of Li's student Luo Zhisong.

菩萨蛮
黄山归来,1984

隔山犹有青山在,
彩云更在群山外。
寻路到云边,
山高亦等闲。

问君何所志,
纵论人间事。
寄愿笔生花,
香飘亿万家。

注:

这首词作于由黄山返回马鞍山市途中。

Tune: Buddha-like Dancers

—Returning from Mount Huangshan, 1984

Hills peep over hills,

Rosy clouds on hills arise.

Finding my way upon the clouds,

Mountains stand tall without bounds.

You ask what ambition I bear,

Human affairs are what I care.

May that my pen like flowers bloom,

Its sweetness wafting to every room.

Note:

This *ci*-lyric was written when Li returned from Mount Huangshan to Ma'anshan.

鹧鸪天
为厉放获得硕士学位作，1985

数载坎坷志未消，
登山且莫问山高。
野无人迹非无路，
村有溪流必有桥。

风飒飒，路迢迢，
但凭年少与勤劳。
倾听江下涛声急，
一代新潮接旧潮。

注：
厉放插队归来，刻苦学习，终于在1985年于中国人民银行总行研究生部获得经济学硕士学位。

Tune: Partridge Sky

—In celebration of Li Fang obtaining Master's Degree, 1985

Years' setbacks cannot alter your will,

Ask not its height when climbing a hill.

A road untrodden is not an impasse,

A rill in the village entails a bridge without fail.

Wind strong, journey long,

Youth and diligence you keep them still.

Swift and pressing are rapids down in the river,

New tides will succeed to the old, be they will or nill.

Note:

After returning from farm work in the countryside, Li Fang spared no pains in studying. Her diligence was finally paid off in 1985 when she obtained master's degree in economics at the Graduate School of People's Bank of China.

浣溪沙
由大连乘轮船到塘沽，1985

大连风狂碧浪高，

津门在望遇新潮，

客船颠簸不停摇。

人世犹如江海渡，

随波起落路迢迢，

不惊不乱靠心桥。

注：

"六五"规划教育经济课题组在大连开会，会议结束后大家一起乘轮船到塘沽，再换长途汽车返回北京。

Tune: Silk-washing Stream

—Journey from Dalian to Tanggu by ship, 1985

Wild wind in Dalian sent blue waves raging high.

When Jinmen was in sight, new tide came by,

Jolting and bumping, the ship could not in rest lie.

Life is like a journey across rivers and sea.

Along the distance long, billows rise and die,

Neither fear nor flutter, hearts linked make a strong tie.

Note:

The "Sixth Five-Year" economic education panel held a meeting in Dalian.

After the meeting, members went to Tanggu by ship, where they took a coach back to Beijing.

踏莎行
于北京大学图书馆整理文稿,1987

戒律清规,
闲人流语,
随风吹过身边去。
藏书楼里作忙人,
楼高那管花飞絮。

不计浮华,
但求警句,
愿将心血其中聚。
清清流水出深山,
须经沙石千回滤。

注:

当时作者正在北大图书馆内整理手稿《非均衡的中国经济》。此书于1990年由经济日报出版社出版,1998年由广东经济出版社再版;2009年由中国大百科全书出版社再版。

Tune: Treading on Grass

—Preparing a manuscript at Peking University Library, 1987

Rules and regulations,

Rumors and gossips,

Away with the wind they pass.

A busy man am I in the tower of books,

Flowers flying outside escape my notice.

Pomposity I care not,

Precept my only compass,

All efforts ready to mass.

Clear water springs from deep mountains, after

A million times' sifting by sands and stones perforce.

Note:

At the time Li was preparing the manuscript of *Chinese Economy in Disequilibrium* at Peking University's library. The book was first published by Economic Daily Press in 1990, and republished by Guangdong Economic Press in 1998 and Encyclopedia of China Publishing House in 2009.

南歌子
为北京大学经济管理系干部班毕业而作,1987

手掌管衙印,
须知百姓情,
犹如晒谷盼秋晴,
最怕连绵细雨下难停。

慎独人人敬,
兼听心内明,
秉公执法似天平,
莫一头偏重一头轻。

注:
北京大学经济管理系是北京大学光华管理学院前身。作者当时是经济管理系主任。

Tune: A Southern Song

—Upon completion of the Cadre Class of Peking University Economic Management Department, 1987

Official seals in hand,

People's conditions in mind.

On grain-drying days pray the autumn sun to reside,

Most dreading drizzles will not end.

Prudent solitude inspires respect in kind,

All-sided listening clears thoughts inside.

Impartially enforce the law like a balance held,

Lest one side be more or less than the other side.

Note:

At the time the author was dean of the Department of Economic Management of Peking University, the predecessor of Guanghua College.

鹊桥仙
看电视剧《红楼梦》，咏贾宝玉，1987

从来受宠，
难逢知己，
利禄远非留意。
有情不解对谁言，
月色冷、一宵怎寐？

此生如梦，
莺声催老，
忍顾落花满地。
人间冤屈恨多多，
无计使、窗前流泪。

注：
看电视剧《红楼梦》之一。

Tune: Immortals on the Magpie Bridge

—A poem for Jia Baoyu, 1987

Pampered from birth,

Confidants hard to meet,

Position and wealth the last of his thought.

To whom he could express his feelings inside?

Cold was the moon, how could he fell asleep?

A dreamlike life he lived,

Hastened by warblers a-chirping,

The sight of ground flower-covered stung his heart.

Human world is full of wrongs, grief and bitterness,

Helpless in front of the window, he could not but weep.

Note:

Poem 1 on the TV series *The Dream of the Red Mansion*.

唐多令
看电视剧《红楼梦》,咏林黛玉,1987

花放漫山红,

叶残万树空,

叹暮秋、卷地西风。

寄寓人家抬冷眼,

世情薄,问行踪?

镜里瘦颜容,

孤身处境同,

燕归来、心事重重。

细雨潇湘难一笑,

谁怜我?梦魂中。

注:

看电视剧《红楼梦》之二。

Tune: Tang Duo Song

—A poem for Lin Daiyu, 1987

Flowers blooming, the whole hill turned red,

Leaves falling, a thousand trees became bald.

Desolate was late autumn, with its all-sweeping west wind.

A lonely lodger was she, cold eyes to meet,

Who cared for her whereabouts, indifferent was the world?

A thin face in the mirror,

The same loneliness as ever.

Swallows returned, her heart laden with care.

In the drizzle Lady Xiaoxiang smiled rare,

Who pitied her? But in dream's snare.

Note:

Poem 2 on the TV series *The Dream of the Red Mansion*.

减字木兰花

看电视剧《红楼梦》,咏薛宝钗,1987

流言常误,

门第姻缘谁做主?

富贵如云,

一阵风来变赤贫。

屋边残雪,

不忍仰看头上月。

苦命相依,

试度寒冬补旧衣。

注:

看电视剧《红楼梦》之三。

Tune: Magnolia in Shortened Form

—A poem for Xue Baochai, 1987

Rumors oft in miscarriage end,

Who can decide marriage family-based?

Wealth and position like clouds instable,

A gust of wind sweeps them all.

Remnant snow lies by the door,

The moon upward makes her heart sore.

Endure hardships together,

Trying to stitch old clothes against cold weather.

Note:

Poem 3 on the TV series *The Dream of the Red Mansion*.

苏幕遮
看电视剧《红楼梦》，咏探春，1987

出名门，
非嫡系，
自律从严，
举止全依礼。
日久园中威自起，
重振家风，
试问谁能替？

雁南飞，
霜满地，
大厦将倾，
挽救空无计。
纵使才高难治理，
远嫁他乡，
有泪人前避。

注：
看电视剧《红楼梦》之四。

Tune: Waterbag Dance

—A poem for Tanchun, 1987

Born a noble,

In a wing-room,

Self-disciplined and strict,

All her conducts conforming to norm.

By and by her dignity in the garden took form,

To revitalize the family vein,

Was there a better claim?

Wild geese flew southward,

The ground coated with rime.

The mansion would topple,

Helpless towards its doom.

With all her talents she resigned in gloom,

Married far,

Withholding tears in a foreign clime.

Note:

Poem 4 on the TV series *The Dream of the Red Mansion*.

巫山一段云
看电视剧《红楼梦》,咏史湘云,1987

官宦门庭在,
名园情意真。
吟诗赏月度青春,
说笑到清晨。

家破终流落,
知音有几个?
江湖飘泊泪留痕,
无语对黄昏。

注:

看电视剧《红楼梦》之五。

Tune: Cloud on Mount Wu

—A poem for Shi Xiangyun, 1987

Rank and mansion sound and safe,

Many a cordial hearts in the Garden ablaze,

Intoning poems in the moonlight on careless days,

Talking and laughing till the first sun rays.

Alas! Home lost, a vagabond turns she!

How many friends could her please?

Wandering in the world, tear stains,

Dusk blurs her speechless gaze.

Note:

Poem 5 on the TV series *The Dream of the Red Mansion*.

少年游

看电视剧《红楼梦》大结局,再咏贾宝玉,1987

家门变故叹无常,
梦醒世情凉。
粗茶剩粥,
零丁孤苦,
破帽破衣裳。

依然冷眼看天下,
不怕笑疏狂。
前去何方?
残雪山村,
一片白茫茫。

注:

看电视剧《红楼梦》之六。

Tune: Wandering While Young

—Another poem for Jia Baoyu, composed after watching the end of the TV series *The Dream of the Red Mansion*, 1987

Family misfortune he gave it a sigh, awakened

To see a world of apathy around.

Coarse tea, leftover porridge,

No money, no friend,

Hat and clothes torn and tattled.

Still he looked at the world with his eyes cold,

Despite being deemed wild.

Where to head?

A village amidst remnant snow,

A vast expanse of whiteness without end.

Note:

Poem 6 on the TV series *The Dream of the Red Mansion*.

卜算子
年终自叙,1987

元月遇寒潮,
惊蛰虫声闹。
只怕春归不再来,
无雨甜桃小。

风紧白云飞,
秋岭丹枫早。
山路从来曲折行,
难免崖边绕。

注:
这正是1987年国内改革形势的写照。

Tune: Song of Divination

—A self-account at year's end, 1987

A cold current smites the first month,

Worms clamor on their Waking days.

My only fear is that spring might not return,

Peaches be small for want of rains.

Clouds fly when wind hastens,

Maples on autumn hills yet in blaze.

Roads on mountains wiggle and wriggle, inevitable

Along the cliff are turns and bends.

Note:

This was a portrayal of domestic reform in 1987.

七古
长沙,湘江桥头,1988

重过湘江人渐老,
难忘去日方年少。
少年气盛未知愁,
坎坷几经盛气收。
而今再到湘江渡,
桥头仍有当时树。
新株老树竞飞花,
江边不见旧人家。

注:

1951年在长沙参加高考时,作者住在岳麓山下湖南大学。每次去长沙城里,须坐两次轮渡(经橘子洲)。1988年夏,作者应中共湖南省委与湖南省人民政府之邀,赴湖南讲学。

A Seven-character Rhymed Poem in Ancient Style

—Xiangjiang Bridge, Changsha, 1988

Once again do I behold Xiangjiang, getting old,

Unforgettable is the day when I left, young and bold.

Sorrow was unknown to me as a man fearless,

Till rounds of setbacks whittled my forwardness.

Once again do I stand here before the river,

Where trees remain on the bridge as ever.

New or old, each vies to bloom and burst,

But gone are riverside families in the past.

Note:

When Li went to Changsha for National College Entrance Examination in 1951, he stayed in Hunan University at the foot of Yuelu Mountain. To get to Changsha downtown, he had to go by ferry twice via Juzizhou. In 1988, Li went to Hunan on a lecture tour at the invitation of Hunan Provincial Committee and People's Government of Hunan.

木兰花

悼念岳母,记1953年送走二女玉春后,
岳母独自留在沅陵家中之事,1988

幼丧慈母春来晚,
未到三旬悲失伴,
领头孤雁往前飞,
阵阵寒风心未乱。

小雏展翅天涯远,
遥望终遭云隔断,
凄凉长夜守秋灯,
整日只将书信盼。

注:

岳母刘宗英,湖南沅陵人,七岁丧母,十六岁出嫁,二十九岁守寡,家境贫寒,借债度日,终将三子二女抚养成人。何玉春是她的二女儿,1953年在沅陵参加高考,进入华中工学院电力系学习。岳母独自留在沅

Tune: Magnolia

—A lament to Mother-in-law, who lived alone in Yuanling after sending off her second daughter Yuchun in 1953, 1988

Spring came late to a child bereaved of mother,
Barely thirty, death tore husband and wife asunder.
Like a lonely wild goose leading children ahead,
Her heart unperturbed against winds bitter.

Birds newly fledged winged their flight yonder,
Afar she looked, clouds dense forbad her endeavor.
By the autumn lamp, into bleak nights long,
Alone she sat, expecting letters coming home forever.

Note:

Liu Zongying, Li's mother-in-law, was a native of Yuanling, Hunan province. Her mother died when she was 7 years old. Married at 16, she was widowed at 29. Being poor, she borrowed money and managed to bring up three sons and

陵家中，两年后（1955年）迁来北京，住在长子何重义家。岳母生于1908年，1988年病逝于北京，享年80岁，葬在北京昌平区佛山公墓。

two daughters. He Yuchun, Li's wife, was her second daughter. After the 1953 National College Entrance Examination in Yuanling, she went to study in the Electric Power Department of Huazhong College of Chemistry. Since then Li's mother-in-law lived alone in Yuanling, until two years later when she came to Beijing and lived with her eldest son He Zhongyi. She died of illness in 1988 at the age of 80, buried in Foshan Cemetery in Changping district, Beijing.

忆秦娥
江苏淮安宝应途中所见,1989

天色早,
两淮塘岸风光好,
风光好,
云开雾散,
绿堤长绕。

农家新置篷船小,
采菱少女双鬓俏,
双鬓俏,
低头荡桨,
抬头微笑。

注:
苏北水乡,别有一番风味。

Tune: Thinking of a Qin Lady

—What I saw in Baoying, Huai'an during my journey in Jiangsu, 1989

Early was the day,
Both sides of the Huai River had a beauty on display,
A beauty on display.
When clouds disappeared and fogs dispersed,
A green bank zigzaged its way.

Small was the fisherman's boat newly bought awhile,
The girl at water chestnuts, pretty was her hair style,
Pretty was her hair style.
She lowered her head to row,
She raised her head in smile.

Note:

Northern Jiangsu is a watery region with a peculiar flavor of its own.

浣溪沙
六十自述，1990

落叶满坡古道迷，
山风萧瑟暗云低，
马儿探路未停蹄。

几度险情终不悔，
一番求索志难移，
此身甘愿作人梯。

注：

这时，作者提出的股份制改革的主张正遭到一些人的批判。

Tune: Silk-washing Stream

—A self-account at the age of 60, 1990

Fallen leaves all over, I lost my way on the ancient road,

Desolate was the mountain wind, low the dark cloud,

My horse searched its way, but never stopped its tread.

Dangers one after another cannot hold me back,

My will to quest the way is not to be altered,

A human ladder I would fain be till life's end.

Note:

At the time Li's proposal to reform the joint-stock system was under attack.

七　律
甘肃酒泉左公柳碑前，1991

雪山南北战云中，
万里征程大漠风。
驰骋铁骑戈壁路，
飞传捷报玉门东。
舍身保国湘军志，
进退运筹主帅功。
回顾当年边塞事，
漫天柳絮赞英雄。

注：

左宗棠率湘军西征，沿途种植杨柳，人称"左公柳"。

A Seven-character Regulated Verse

—Before the tabular of Zuo Zongtang in Jiuquan, Gansu, 1991

War clouds enfolded north and south of the snow mountain,

Ten thousand miles they journeyed to the gusty terrain.

Cavalries on horseback galloped on the Gobi desert vast,

Report of victory to speed till East Jade Gate they did attain.

To sacrifice for the country was the will of Xiang troop to retain,

To withdraw or attack was the feat of its Captain to ordain.

In recollection of events on the frontier over years past,

Catkins whirled in the sky in praise of the hero on their domain.

Note:

When he led the Xiang troop along the westward expedition, Zuo Zongtang planted willows all the way, which were then nicknamed "Revered Mr. Zuo's willows", i.e., willows planted by the Revered Mr. Zuo.

七　律

从图书馆借得王沂孙《碧山乐府》，读后有感，1991

动天豪气荡无存，
人世真情剩几分？
纵有心声应暗蓄，
何须晦涩不留痕。
铺陈仿佛南朝赋，
堆砌绝非两宋魂。
恕我才疏难领悟，
一声长叹又黄昏。

注：

王沂孙，宋末元初词人。

A Seven-character Regulated Verse

—Reading *Collected Poems of Green Mountains* by Wang Yisun, borrowed from the library, 1991

Vanished is heroic spirit that Heaven doth rock,

What remains of genuine feelings in the world?

Heartfelt wishes should be implicit, if any,

Why obscure and vague, not to be found?

Lengthy like rhapsodies of the Southern dynasty,

Fancy phrases alien to two Songs in them abound.

My limited scope falters in such profundity,

With a long sigh, I see dusk once more around.

Note:

Wang Yisun, a *ci*-lyric writer in the late Song and early Yuan dynasty.

七 律
虎门炮台，1992

无奈权臣只徇私，
边情火急几人知。
名园歌舞升平夜，
江下官兵浴血时。
割地终成千古恨，
改弦引发万民思。
回归之日再凭吊，
前事不忘后事师。

注：

此时距香港回归还有五年。

A Seven-character Regulated Verse

—Humen Port, 1992

Alas! Authority was abused by many a minister,

Whoever knew the dire urgency in the frontier?

Songs and dances continued to celebrate good times,

Soldiers and officers fought to death down the river.

When territories were ceded to become a lifetime regret,

The reform of regime caused the nation to ponder.

Bear this in mind on the day of return,

Success depends on lessons learnt from past failure.

Note:

At the time there were five years to go before Hong Kong's return to China.

七　律
湖南芷江抗战胜利受降纪念碑坊，1992

今日有缘返故城，

当年情景又重生。

路人相遇传佳讯，

陋巷通宵爆竹声。

游子慢吟工部句，

乡亲难禁泪珠横。

休谈往事随风去，

血字牌坊血砌成。

注：

1945年8月，日本宣布无条件投降之日，作者正在湘西沅陵。当时的狂欢情景，至今仍在脑海之中。芷江受降纪念牌坊，外形像一"血"字。

A Seven-character Regulated Verse

—A memorial arch of Japanese surrender in Zhijiang, Hunan, 1992

It must be fate I came back to this old town,
When before me past events resurfaced.
Passersby shouted good news to each other,
All night through in mean alleys fireworks not ceased.
People away from home intoned verses of Du Fu,
Country fellows could not help their tears constant.
Do not say things bygone will vanish like wind,
The "blood-shaped" monument was blood-built.

Note:

In August 1945 when Japan declared unconditional surrender, Li was in Yuanling in western Hunan. The wild excitement at the time is still fresh in his mind. The memorial arch in Zhijiang is in the shape of the Chinese character "血", meaning blood.

鹧鸪天

游浙江定海普陀山,

船中闻邻座几位民营企业家闲谈有感,1993

大道尽头小道弯,
游人许愿到仙山,
乐施好善修功德,
自律从严心始安。

生命短,海天宽,
隔厢妙语可通禅:
若无信仰为支柱,
名利场中行路难。

注:

普陀山,与五台山、峨眉山、九华山并列为中国佛教四大圣地。本词最后两句,值得深思。

Tune: Partridge Sky

—Touring Mount Putuo in Zhejiang by boat, overhearing several private entrepreneurs' casual talk, 1993

At the end of a road a small path winds away,

Travelers come to the fairy mountain to pray.

Good deeds build up merits and virtues,

Peace in mind compels strict discipline to obey.

Short is life, broad the sea and sky,

Witty talk next door illuminates a Buddhist way:

Devoid of belief as a pillar in life,

Procession in the Vanity Fair will be no easy play.

Note:

Wutai Mountain, Jiuhua Mountain, Mount Putuo and Mount Emei are named together as the four Buddhist Shrines in China. The last two lines deserve deep thinking.

减字木兰花
——结婚三十六周年，在海南三亚，1994

海风拂面，
往事如烟飘已远。
回忆心伤，
今日犹疑在梦乡。

是真非梦，
眼见亭边枝叶动。
琼岛新城，
携手天涯听浪声。

注：
此时女儿厉放在澳大利亚莫纳石大学攻读博士学位，儿子厉伟在深圳工作。

Tune: Magnolia in Shortened Form

—Commemorating the 36th wedding anniversary in Sanya, Hainan, 1994

Sea wind kisses our faces,

Past events fade away like puffs of incenses.

Recollection stings the heart,

Even today I doubt it was a dream I dreamt.

It IS true,

See branches beside the pavilion sway fro and to.

A new city in Hainan Island,

At earth's end we listen to waves sounding hand in hand.

Note:

At the time Li's daughter Li Fang pursued her doctorial degree at Monash University in Australia, and his son Li Wei worked in Shenzhen.

南歌子
母亲去世后整理旧相册，翻到我婴儿100天时的照片，伤感万分，1995

追忆摇篮曲，
泪流有几多。
秋凉无语对星河，
旧事犹新终夜不消磨。

梦里微微笑，
甜甜小酒窝。
醒来咿呀学儿歌，
当日那知慈母苦奔波。

注：

作者的母亲袁是琳因心脏病于1995年8月19日在北京安贞医院去世，终年84岁。

Tune: A Southern Song

—Sorting out an old album after Mother's death, immensely sick at heart when seeing my 100-day photo, 1995

Recalling childhood lullabies,

Tears dimmed my sight.

Speechless, I looked up at the star-spangled sky,

Memories flooded into the sleepless cold autumn night.

A gentle smile in dreams,

Two sweet dimples in delight.

In wakened hours nursery rhymes babbled I,

Mother's toil was the least of my childish thought.

Note:

The author's mother, Yuan Shilin, died of a heart attack in Anzhen Hospital on August 19, 1995, aged 84.

渔歌子
福建泰宁，1996

两岸青山雾渐收，

春江水碧小蓬舟，

蕉叶绿，

柳丝柔，

一生几次画中游？

注：

泰宁，闽西山区的一个县。

Tune: A Fisherman's Song

—Taining, Fujian, 1996

Green hills on both sides slowly come off their misty coat,

Small caravan boats on the emerald spring water float.

Plantain leaves verdant,

Willow twigs soft,

How many times can one travel in a painting's feast?

Note:

Taining is a county in the mountainous region in western Fujian.

唐多令
过河南朱仙镇,1996

回首倍苍茫,
路边送夕阳,
霎时间、皓月如霜,
秀色难掩千载恨,
翻宋史,总心凉。

战地野花香,
金牌更感伤,
小商河、水已浑黄,
眼底汴京难再到,
英雄泪,一行行。

注:

朱仙镇,岳飞收到金牌,退兵之处。

Tune: Tang Duo Song

—Passing Zhuxian county in Henan, 1996

Looking back, vastness doubled,

The sun set off on the roadside.

All at once, the bright moon came out frost-cold,

But beauty could not conceal remorse long-held,

Browsing the history of Song, chill was I inside.

Wild flowers sweetened the battlefield,

Sorrow aggravated before the medal gold.

The water in Xiaoshang river was already yellow-tainted,

Bianjing at eye's sight, no more could it be reached,

Hero's tears came down, in lines uninterrupted.

Note:

Zhuxian county is the place where Yue Fei received the golden medal to withdraw.

调笑令
为厉澳两周岁题照,1997

春雨,

春雨,

小树长高几许?

今朝犹绕膝前,

转眼翩翩少年。

年少,

年少,

处处天涯芳草。

注:

厉澳两周岁时,厉放自澳大利亚寄来彩照,作者特为小外孙照片题词。

Tune: Song of Flirtation

—A poem for Li Ao's 2nd birthday photo, 1997

Spring rain,

Spring rain,

What height does the little tree gain?

Today a toddler around the knees,

Tomorrow a young man at ease.

Young age,

Young age,

Fragrant grasses are everywhere on life's stage.

Note:

When Li Ao was two years old, Li Fang sent back his photo from Australia. Li wrote this poem especially for that occasion.

南乡子
为母亲扫墓，1997

悬念几时休，
谁解慈颜整日愁，
孙辈散居千里外，
心忧，
恨不分身到五洲。

碑下泪难收，
往事如梭去复留，
母逝方知儿也老，
飕飕，
黄叶随风掠过头。

注：
作者的母亲袁是琳于1995年病逝，葬于北京昌平佛山公墓。

Tune: Song of a Southern Country

—Sweeping Mother's tomb, 1997

When did her worry cease?

Who could read the sorrow on her kind face?

Grandchildren scattering wide apart,

Heart anxious,

She would fain be split to five continents apiece.

Beneath the tomb tears fall endless,

Past events flash by and back, restless.

Alas! Mother passed away, I grow old,

Wind rustles,

Yellow leaves my head fly across.

Note:

The author's mother, Yuan Shilin, died of illness in 1995, and was buried in Foshan Cemetery in Changping district, Beijing.

减字木兰花
贺厉放获博士学位,1998

艰辛历尽,

风雨当年凭自信。

更上层楼,

莫让时光似水流。

扬鞭再赶,

创业从来无早晚。

处世唯谦,

天外须知还有天。

注:

为厉放获得澳大利亚莫纳石大学博士学位而作。

Tune: Magnolia in Shortened Form

—In congratulation of Li Fang obtaining a doctorial degree, 1998

Many a hardship gone through,

Wind and rain your confidence did prove.

A layer still higher,

Do not let time flow by like water.

A whiplash for a new journey,

To start an undertaking there is no late or early.

Modesty be the only code,

For peaks arise on peaks attained.

Note:

Li Fang obtained her doctorial degree of Monash University in Australia. This poem was written in congratulation of that event.

钗头凤
记厉莎周岁，1999

粉裙裤，花间路，
晃摇迈出人生步。
杏红腮，笑容开，
不须牵手，
试上阶台，
乖！乖！乖！

望高处，飞尘雾，
未来当学常青树。
畅胸怀，自成材，
漫长年月，
怎做安排，
猜！猜！猜！

注：
1999年7月16日为厉莎一周岁。作者特地为小孙女填了这首《钗头凤》。

Tune: Phoenix Hairpin

—In celebration of Li Sha's first birthday, 1999

In pantskirt pink, among flowers thick,

A toddler makes her life's first walk.

Her cheeks rosy, her smiles sunny,

Without a helping hand,

Upstairs she tries hardy,

Lovely, lovely, lovely!

Looking high, dust on the fly,

Be modeled on evergreens by and by.

Keep an open stance, success is a matter of course,

In years to come,

What will be her choice?

Guess, guess, guess!

Note:

Li Sha was one year old on July 16, 1999. This poem was specially written for her.

破阵子
七十感怀，2000

往日悲歌非梦，
平生执着追寻。
纵说琼楼难有路，
盼到来年又胜今，
好诗莫自吟。

纸上应留墨迹，
书山总有知音。
处世长存宽厚意，
行事唯求无愧心，
笑游桃李林。

注：

作者七十岁生日那一天，历届弟子数百人在北京大学光华管理学院聚会庆祝，作者以本词答谢。

Tune: Dance of the Calvary

—Written upon my 70th birthday, 2000

Past elegies are not an illusion,

Consistently I search my way.

The road to jade tower is hard to find,

But the coming year promises a better day,

Do not alone sing a lay.

Paper should be inked,

In the pursuit of knowledge friends will for you stay.

Always cherish a broad and kind heart,

Naught but a clear conscience to obey,

To roam a garden merry and gay.

Note:

On his 70th birthday, hundreds of Li's students gathered at Guanghua College of Peking University in celebration. Li wrote this poem in acknowledgement.

柳梢青
过宁夏固原有感,2002

未到寒霜,
漫山半秃,
田野枯黄。
烽火多年,
重灾不绝,
留下凄凉。

难寻昔日风光,
古通道、繁华汉唐。
盛景堪追,
雄姿犹在,
巍巍城墙。

注:

固原,一直是西北重镇,今已衰败。

Tune: Green Willow Twigs

—Passing Guyuan in Ningxia, 2002

Before frost falls cold,

Half of the mountain is bold,

The field a withered scene to behold.

Continuous war fire,

Grave disaster nonstop,

Conspired to wreak a distress untold.

Past grandeur nowhere to be found,

Ancient passages glories of Han and Tang unfold.

Splendours untraceable,

Majestic stance remains,

So long as lofty walls stand.

Note:

Guyuan has long been a major town in northwest China, but is on the wane today.

鹧鸪天
瑞士洛桑古迹,2002

天纵有情心也偏,
人生不信只由天,
何须计较沉浮事,
褒贬从来一阵烟。

山涧过,是平原,
秋游且到小溪边,
甘泉无语流千里,
沙土飞扬弹指间。

注:

洛桑,瑞士故城,位于日内瓦湖北岸。

Tune: Partridge Sky

—Historical site of Lausanne, Sweden, 2002

If Heaven had a feeling heart it will lose balance,

But life will not submit to Heaven's dominance.

Needless to care about ups and downs,

Pros and cons like a puff of smoke go without trace.

The plain lies ahead, when creeks got across,

Go to the rill to court autumn's pace.

Soundless the spring flows a thousand miles,

Sand and dust fly away but in transience.

Note:

Lausanne is an ancient city in Sweden, to the north of Lake Geneva.

鹧鸪天
回鞍山,代何玉春作,2003

垂柳新荷水盈盈,

啼声几处听黄莺。

湖光已使游人醉,

山色更添诗画情。

招手唤,笑声迎,

故交叙旧短长亭。

谁家又放蓝桥曲,

勾起当年心不平。

注:

何玉春离开鞍山已33年,此次携外孙厉澳(八岁)、孙女厉莎(五岁)重来。

Tune: Partridge Sky

—Returning to Anshan, written on behalf of He Yuchun, 2003

Willows, new lotus, full water,

Warblers chirping hither and thither.

The lake alone already intoxicates its viewers,

Mountains lavish it more with a poetic flavor.

A wave of hand, a smile in answer,

Friends chat over old times at pavilions far and near.

Whence comes the woeful parting song?

Arousing memories which my heart stir.

Note:

After 33 years' absence, He Yuchun returned to Anshan along with Grandson Li Ao (8 years old) and Granddaughter Li Sha (5 years old).

洞仙歌

为厉放四十五岁、厉伟四十岁而作,2003

弟顽姐护,

幼时情难表,

陋巷危房度年少。

浪中游、不问前站遥遥,

惊回首,

往事如今缥缈。

南国花未谢,

碧海青山,

云下烟波接芳草。

暮雨正潇潇,

桥跨罗湖,

秋凉去、香江春早。

课子女,

日夜识辛劳。

Tune: Song of a Fairy in the Cave

—Written upon Li Fang's 45th and Li Wei's 40th birthdays, 2003

Naughty brother, caring sister,

Unable to express feelings as a toddler,

In shabby lanes and a house dilapidated their childhood spent.

Waves they rode on, disregarding the distance long or short,

Until startled,

To see past events filmy in retrospect.

In the southern land flowers bloom still,

The sea is blue, mountains green,

Misty water below clouds extends to grass sweet.

In pattering rain at twilight,

A bridge spans Luohu Lake.

Cold autumn gone, Xiangjiang River is already a vernal sight.

Admonishing daughter and son,

Toiling day and night.

念父母当初,

掌灯严教。

注:

2003年11月30日,作者夫妇、女儿厉放一家、儿子厉伟一家,在香港聚会,庆祝厉放四十五岁、厉伟四十岁生日。

Unforgettable was mother and father,
Strict by the lamplight.

Note:

On November 30, 2003, the author and his wife, their daughter Li Fang and her family, their son Li Wei and his family, gathered in Hongkong to celebrate Li Fang's 45th and Li Wei's 40th birthdays.

虞美人
山东荣成市成山头，2004

少年观海天无际，
故土绵绵意。
轻舟好去莫回头，
破浪直前随处有芳洲。

老来得失应知矣，
潮退潮升起。
一番秋雨一番风，
换得心宽南北亦西东。

注：
成山头在山东半岛最东端。

Tune: The Beautiful Lady Yu

—At Chengshantou in Rongcheng, Shandong, 2004

When young, boundless was the sky over sea,

Affectionate was the land nursing me.

Boarding a boat for a trip not to return,

Waves surging, I saw, fragrant islet lie on every turn.

In old age gains and losses will be clear,

As tide falls and rises year after year.

A bout of autumn rain, a puff of wind,

North and south are the same as west and east to a broad mind.

Note:

Chengshantou is on the east end of Shandong peninsular.

清平乐
甘肃崆峒山,2004

台阶几许,
百鸟啾啾语。
万物竞生来又去,
无序悠然有序。

雨停始见莺飞,
花开全赖风微。
乐业安居处处,
有为出自无为。

注:
崆峒山,在平凉境内,是道教名山。

Tune: Pure Serene Music

—Kongtong Mountain, Gansu, 2004

Where do steps stop?

A hundred birds chirp.

Myriad creatures race to come and go without letup,

Order in disorder lies deep.

Warblers fly when rain stays,

Flowers bloom when wind fades.

Everywhere is a scene of full contentment,

A deed completes itself when no deed aids.

Note:

Kongtong Mountain is a famous Taoist mountain in Pingliang, Gansu.

踏莎行
重到济南，2004

关注民生，
不忘少取，
乡间兴旺因多予。
近郊已是小康村，
山区喜说机难遇。

泉水轻声，
情人细语，
广场起舞农家女。
稼轩清照若归来，
挥毫定有惊人句。

注：

李清照、辛弃疾（稼轩）都是济南人。

Tune: Treading on Grass

—Revisiting Jinan, 2004

Attend to civil life,

Forget not less taking,

Rural prosperity depends on more giving.

Villages fairly-off already bestrew the outskirts,

People jocundly acclaim the opportunity as a blessing.

Springs softly gurgling,

Lovers gently murmuring,

Country girls in the square dancing.

If Jiaxuan and Qingzhao returned to life,

Brush in hand, they would dash off lines startling.

Note:

Li Qingzhao and Xin Qiji (Jiaxuan) were both natives of Jinan.

七 律
从教五十周年暨七十五岁生日自叙,2005

秋霜染得漫山红,
看叶登高叠叠峰。
昔日荒沙连大漠,
今朝道畔尽花丛。
多年劳累非虚掷,
往事堪思一笑中。
鬓白不为闲话扰,
加鞭纵马对西风。

注:

2005年12月3日,北京大学光华管理学院为作者从教五十周年暨七十五周岁生日举行庆祝会。

A Seven-character Regulated Verse

—A self-account on the 50th anniversary of my teaching career & 75th birthday, 2005

The whole mountain was dyed red by autumn frost,

Peak after peak I climbed for a view of leaves radiant.

In old time a land of sand towards desert vast,

Now with flowers clustering the road is vibrant.

Labor is not lost on years' hard toil,

I smile at past events in retrospect.

Grey-templed and immune to evil tongues,

I spurn my horse against wind from the west.

Note:

On December 3, 2005, Guanghua College of Peking University held a party to celebrate the 50th anniversary of Li's teaching career and his 75th birthday.

踏莎行
江西婺源农村所见,2006

草密林深,
莺飞蝶舞,
野花开遍溪边渡。
山乡无处不桃源,
粉墙黛瓦谁家住?

淳朴民风,
勤劳农户,
排排屋后新茶树。
窗明院净客人来,
炖鸡香满村前路。

注:

婺源县,原属安徽徽州府,今属江西上饶市。

Tune: Treading on Grass

—A view of the countryside in Wuyuan, Jiangxi, 2006

Grass thick, forest dense,

Birds fly, butterflies flutter,

Wild flowers bloom the stream all over.

Every place is a heaven in the countryside,

Who cares to be a white-wall and black-vale dweller?

Simple is their lifestyle,

Diligent every farmer,

At the back of their house rows of new tea glitter.

Windows and yards await guests on their best look,

The country road brims with stewed chicken on the cooker.

Note:

The county of Wuyuan belonged to Huizhou in olden times. Now it is under the jurisdiction of Shangrao, Jiangxi.

一剪梅
结婚四十九年,代何玉春作,2007

绿树遮阴道道弯,
过了山峦,
还是山峦。
从来一路不孤单。
雨水潺潺,
溪水潺潺。

跋涉多年未觉寒,
公事虽难,
家事更难。
小姑妯娌总相安,
穷也心宽,
累也心宽。

注:
作者为长兄,下面有弟弟五人,妹妹四人。

Tune: A Twig of Plum Blossoms

—The 49th wedding anniversary, written on behalf of He Yuchun, 2007

Green trees blocking the sun, bend after bend,

A mountain climbed,

Another continued.

Never was I alone on the road,

The rain babbled,

The stream babbled.

Trudging for years, never felt I cold,

Public affairs were hard,

Family affairs more than hard.

Sisters-in-law got on well as of old,

In poverty a broad mind,

In fatigue a broad mind.

Note:

The author is the eldest of the family, with five younger brothers, and four younger sisters.

满庭芳
北京大学110周年校庆，2008

风雨维新，

激流五四，

红楼岁月留痕。

八年烽火，

跋涉到边村。

百载弦歌未绝，

传科学、民主精神。

怀先烈，

神州大地，

何处祭英魂？

新人！

追往昔，

心中暗誓，

济世经纶。

定勤读寒窗，

迎送星辰。

Tune: Courtyard Full of Fragrance

—In celebration of Peking University's 110th anniversary, 2008

Reforming wind and rain,

Torrents of the May Fourth,

The Red Building bears all time's imprint.

During the eight-year war fire,

To the village boarder we treked.

The hundred-year-old moral education is not ended,

The spirit of science and democracy we consistently promote.

Recalling souls heroic,

On the land of magic,

Where is their place of rest?

New generation!

Retrace the past,

To promise at heart,

Helping the country with statecraft.

Study hard in spite of adversity,

Early in the day and deep into night;

朝夕湖光塔影，

离毕业、几度冬春。

争相勉，

兴亡重任，

我辈主乾坤。

注：

北京大学成立于1898年。到2008年，已成立110周年。

From dawn to dusk, the mirrored pagoda by the side,

Full cycles of season to witness till studies complete.

Encourage each other,

On every shoulder,

Weighs the country's fate!

Note:

Founded in 1898, Peking University has gone through 110 years by 2008.

清平乐
记慧慧、嘉嘉100天，2008

海风频送，

天赐龙和凤，

姐姐笑中成美梦，

弟弟醒来好动。

西墙挂满花枝，

东墙遍贴诗词，

莫道才经百日，

人间乐趣初知。

注：

慧慧和嘉嘉，是厉伟、崔京涛夫妇在香港所生的一对龙凤胎。

Tune: Pure Serene Music

—Lines composed to mark Huihui and Jiajia being 100 days old, 2008

Sea wind frequently blows,

A dragon and phoenix Heaven endows,

Elder sister smiles as her dream grows,

Younger brother forever is on his toes.

A wall of flowers on the west,

A gamut of poems on the east,

Say not but a hundred days past,

Life's joys they have begun to taste.

Note:

Huihui and Jiajia are a pigeon pair of Li Wei and Cui Jingtao born in Hong Kong.

七　绝
内蒙乌拉特中旗秦长城遗址，2009

渠北渠南好牧场，

山前草绿葵花黄，

秦兵泉下应宽慰，

塞上和谐富裕乡。

注：

牧户农户相处很好，边境安定无忧。

A Seven-character Quatrain

—The site of Qin-state Great Wall in Urad Middle Banner in Inner Mongolia, 2009

On the south and north of the ditch are pastures mellow,
In front of the hills grass is green, sunflowers are yellow.
Qin soldiers may lie in relief on their beds underground:
Life on the frontier follows a wealthy and harmonious flow.

Note:

People get on well with each other on the border, living in a state of carefree stability.

木兰花
题重庆市武隆县仙女山镇,2010

野花香绕溪边树,
泉水纷飞升薄雾,
当年仙女下凡来,
暂定武隆休息处。

画廊百里乌江渡,
夹壁谷底芳草路,
有缘仙女又重游,
偏选武隆长久住。

注:

重庆武隆,著名风景区。

Tune: Magnolia

—Fairy Mountain town at Wulong county, Chongqing, 2010

Wild flowers perfume trees alongside the stream,

Spring water splashes into a misty film.

The fairy lady came down on earth,

Choosing Wulong as her place to dream.

Wujiang unveils a-hundred-*li* scroll without seam,

Between cliffs and down valleys lies a grassy realm.

Fate has it that the lady paid her second patronage,

And chose to stay here for life on a benevolent whim.

Note:

Wulong in Chongqing is a famous scenic spot.

七　绝

烟台养马岛，
秦始皇东巡时将此岛辟为养马场，2010

东莱遗址早无踪，
崖下涛声代代同，
游客已忘封禅事，
秦皇只在戏文中。

注：
胶东，古东莱国所在地。

A Seven-character Quatrain

—Horse Island in Yantai, which Qinshihuang reserved for horse-keeping during his eastward journey, 2010

The site of Donglai is traceless already,

The tide under cliff sings the same melody,

Travelers have forgotten the ceremony of worship,

Searching Emperor Qin in operas only.

Note:

Jiaodong is the site of Donglai in ancient times.

浣溪沙

莎士比亚故居(英国牛津郡莎士比亚故居,遇见外地来此演出的小剧团),2012

道具随身处处家,
篷车路窄陷平沙,
剧团朝暮走天涯。

每遇节假观众聚,
院墙内外扎红花,
竹椅围坐伴飞霞。

注:
莎士比亚故居已成为群众戏剧演出的中心,几乎每天都有戏剧上演。

Tune: Silk-washing Stream

—Meeting a non-local troupe at Shakespeare's former residence in Oxford, 2012

Props on hand, home was on every land,

Road narrow, the van trapped in flat sand,

Morn and night, their feet knew no end.

On festivals and holidays people convened,

Inside and outside the wall flowers bloomed red,

Bamboo chairs in a ring, rosy clouds flying ahead.

Note:

Shakespeare's former residence has become a center of theatrical performance.

There are plays on show almost every day.

七　绝
为北京大学光华管理学院校友返校日作，2012

楼前幼树是谁栽？

窗下依然旧绿苔。

往事如丝犹可忆，

新花正盼燕归来。

注：

光华管理学院的前身是经济管理系，成立于1985年，至2012年已经27年。

A Seven-character Quatrain

—Lines composed on Guanghua College of Peking University Alumni Day, 2012

Small trees in front of the building, who planted them?

Below the window mosses grow as in old time.

Memories of my boyish days trickle in,

Newborn flowers anticipate swallows' journey home.

Note:

Founded in 1985, Guanghua College developed from the former Department of Economic Management. By 2012 it has been in existence for 27 years.

踏莎行
第七次赴贵州毕节扶贫有感，2012

积雪消融，

山林甦醒，

纵横百里黄花影。

杜鹃绽放漫坡红，

春风已过乌蒙岭。

村镇繁荣，

家和院静，

财源通畅无他径。

艰辛创业信为先，

人人学艺开新境。

注：

作者自2003年担任贵州毕节试验区专家顾问组组长，2009年改任贵州毕节试验区总顾问以来，到2012年为止，先后七次到毕节市各县区进行扶贫调研。

Tune: Treading on Grass

—Lines composed upon my 7th journey to Bijie in Guizhou under the anti-poverty programme, 2012

Snow melts away,

Forest wakes up,

A hundred miles of yellow flowers stretch nonstop.

Azaleas burst and bloom until the whole slope is red-dyed,

Spring has breezed its way across Wumeng's top.

Villages and towns in prosperity,

Households in serene harmony's lap,

Wealth in continuance has a single course to map.

Hard enterprise begins with credence,

Everyone learns a feat, a new field to reap.

Note:

From Li's designation as head of the consultation team for Bijie pilot programme in 2003, and general consultant of the same programme in 2009, to the year 2012, he had went on seven trips to different counties and districts in Bijie for poverty-concerned issues.

鹧鸪天
四川广安邓小平故里，2013

千里嘉陵古渡头，

少年江岸念全球，

简装从此天涯去，

一别家乡八十秋。

山不老，水长流，

三回起落志难酬。

多亏雾散阳光现，

力挽狂澜济九州。

注：

邓小平从广安辗转赴法国工读后，据说忙于国事，从未回到广安。

Tune: Partridge Sky

—Guang'an, hometown of Deng Xiaoping, 2013

Along the thousand-*li* Jialing, before the ferry old,

A youth stood by the riverside, his heart clung to the world,

From whence simple equipped, far and wide he went,

For the space of eighty autumns without a trip round.

Hills remain young, water will not end,

Unfulfilled was his will, though rise and fall thrice withstood.

Happily the fog was gone and sun reappeared,

A strenuous move he launched to save the land.

Note:

It is said that after he managed to go from Guang'an to France on a work-study programme, Deng Xiaoping, the duty-bound man, hadn't returned to Guang'an since.

七 绝
三清山，2014

婺绿鹃红缀玉山，
鄱阳南下几重关，
林深问道道何在，
天地人生正气间。

注：

三清山，道教圣地，在今江西省上饶市玉山境内。婺源茶绿、杜鹃花红，是上饶美景。

A Seven-character Quatrain

—Sanqing Mountain, 2014

Jade Mountain sparkles in green tea and azalea red,
How many are the passes down Poyang southward?
Asking the Way in forest deep, —where does it lie?
Between the vital energy of Heaven and Earth we stand.

Note:

Sanqing Mountain is a holy place for Taoists, in the Jade Mountain of Shangrao, Jiangxi province. Green tea and red azalea in Wuyuan are divine views peculiar to Shangrao.

鹧鸪天
《厉以宁诗词全集》整理完毕,有感而作,2017

独坐书斋天地宽,

推窗始觉在人间。

山头新月匆匆去,

留下青松夜夜寒。

挥笔易,

治贫难,

几家愁苦几家欢。

诗词岂止闲情诉,

广厦城乡大众安。

Tune: Partridge Sky

—Upon completion of *The Complete Poetry of Li Yining*, 2017

Alone I sit in the study, broad is earth and sky,

I open the window, the world meets my eye.

The crescent moon on hill's top hurries away,

Leaving pines alone in cold nights standing high.

Composition is easy,

Solution hard to come by.

Some in distress sigh, some in comfort lie.

Poems involve more than sentimental lay,

But the wellbeing of every household far and nigh.

洙泗濠濮，松柏桐椿（编后记）
——记厉以宁著作外译，并祝先生九秩寿辰

吴 浩

一

仍然记得我对北京大学最初也是最为深刻的印象，来自1998年5月我在徽州腹地休宁中学图书馆阅读《南风窗》杂志的惊鸿一瞥。彼时正值北大一百周年校庆，美国总统克林顿访问中国并在北大办公楼礼堂发表演讲为北大庆生。作为一个徽州县城没有见过世面的青涩男孩，第一次见到铜版彩色新闻纸印制的精美杂志，无论是图像抑或文字都深深震撼了心灵。那一期的《南风窗》不啻北大校庆专刊，系统比较了北大清华的异同，还介绍了北大一百年来的风雨兼程，厉以宁先生的道德事功文章深深打动了我。我在心底默念：微斯人，吾谁与归？

彼时正值高一年级下学期，面临文理分科选择的烦恼——我的文科理科都还不错，都很有希望考上北大清华。

但正因为这次邂逅,正是厉以宁先生人格魅力的感召,在1998年那个夏日的黄昏,我做出了人生的抉择——选择文科,报考北京大学,最理想的当然是考上光华管理学院,亲炙厉以宁先生的教诲。

2000年的高考,我考出了理想的分数,要先估分后报志愿。我毅然决然地报考北京大学,但对于具体专业的选择,却有着不同的声音。我矢志报考光华管理学院,光华在安徽招生的具体专业是金融——那时候互联网尚未普及,山区县城无论是老师还是家长对中国高等教育的高峰都是一头雾水——我特别敬重的教导主任也是全国特级教师,劝我不要报考金融,说金融有什么好,出来就是在银行干事情;我说那我报北大中文系呢,教导主任说中文系出来就是当秘书;父亲为我参谋,还是报国际政治吧,当个外交官挺风光。

我后来阴错阳差上了北大国际政治系,但做厉以宁先生门生的朴素愿望一直深藏心底。到北大报到后不久,厉以宁先生给大一新生做报告,早早去占位置听讲,没想到办公楼礼堂早已被挤得水泄不通。我挨着办公楼礼堂的墙根听完了厉先生一个多小时的报告,仍然记得厉先生引用《吕氏春秋》的典故,讲了"子贡赎人"和"子路受牛"的故事。厉以宁先生深入浅出地讲这两个故事,醉翁之意不在酒,意在探讨民营经济在改革进程中所面临的制度、观念、激励等多方面的因素。厉先生对中国现实问题的关切和对中国传统文化的精通,给我留下了深刻印象。

二

2006年，我从北大硕士毕业，到北外机关工作。时任北外校长郝平教授出身北大，对厉以宁先生非常敬重。厉先生欣然答应北外的邀请，担任北外哲学社会科学学院名誉院长，并多次来北外做报告。2009年春天，我从北外机关调到外研社工作，有幸主持厉以宁先生文集的英译出版。这部文集精选了厉以宁先生在1980到1998年之间发表的关于中国经济改革与发展的16篇代表性著述，其中心指导思想是：改革与转型服务于经济增长与社会发展；经济增长和社会发展服务于社会普通公民的福祉。这些著述在发表时都对彼时的中国经济实践产生了广泛而深远的影响，代表了改革开放成功实践背后中国经济学派的理论贡献。也正因此，这部文集不仅是厉先生学术思想演变的写照，更展现了中国经济改革与发展的宏大历程。

外研社对英译厉先生这部文集非常重视，由著名翻译家凌原教授担任主译，并就其中一些专业问题的翻译与北大光华管理学院蔡洪滨教授、周黎安教授等反复讨论磋商，同时请澳大利亚专家对语言进行润色定稿。

2010年11月，恰逢厉以宁先生八十华诞，厉先生这部经济学文集的英译版以《中国经济改革发展之路》（*Economic Reform and Development: The Chinese Way*）之名正式出版，厉先生的学生、英国社会科学院院士、伦敦大学亚非学院金融管理系首席教授孙来祥为文集作序。

为什么厉以宁先生对这部文集冠以"中国经济改革发展之路"之名？异曲同工的是，为什么为厉先生祝寿的学术研讨会也取名为"经济学理论和中国道路"？厉先生和我们谈道："我不用'中国模式'，因为'模式'往往是固定化的；我用'中国道路'，因为它更容易博采众长。中国改革开放所走出的道路，不仅借鉴了外国经验，也吸收了自己的经验教训，是'谁有优点就学谁'。"那时正是"中国模式"的提法风靡一时之日，厉以宁先生以经济学家的敏锐葆有冷静的头脑，坚持"中国道路"的概念。2012年秋，党的十八大报告中提出了"道路自信、理论自信、制度自信"三个自信的理论，厉以宁先生倡导的"中国道路"的理论范式为"道路自信"提供了学术参考。

《中国经济改革发展之路》英译版推出之后，很快受剑桥大学出版社青睐。剑桥大学出版社第一时间引进版权，收入剑桥大学出版社"剑桥中国文库"（The Cambridge China Library）丛书。2012年4月16日，剑桥大学出版社专门于伦敦举办了该书海外版的首发仪式。我有幸随厉以宁先生、厉先生夫人何玉春师母和车耳学长等赴英国出席首发式。厉以宁先生在首发式上做了题为《双重转型和中国道路》的主旨演讲。厉先生在演讲中总结经济转型的"中国道路"："中国进行的经济转型实际上是双重转型。一是从传统农业社会向工业社会、现代社会的转型；二是从计划经济体制向市场经济的转型。这两种经济转型在中国是重叠在一起了。二者同样重要,同样决定着中国的命运。"

我在泰晤士河畔的会场聆听厉先生的报告,想起了剑桥大学出版社曾经出版过的《剑桥中国史》系列和李约瑟博士主编的《中国科学技术史》系列,这两部中国主题的经典著作都是海外汉学家直接用英语写成。厉以宁先生的英译作品纳入"剑桥中国文库"出版,从中国学术著作对外传播而言,有着开创性的意义。厉先生的演讲和着泰晤士河的波涛,拍打着我的心灵,我也隐隐感觉到时代的脉动。

三

厉以宁先生关于中国经济体制改革的理论创新遍及多个领域,他在股份制改革、国有企业产权制度改革和证券法、非公经济36条以及非公经济新36条等经济法规的制订方面都做出了历史性的贡献。在去年庆祝改革开放40周年大会上,厉以宁先生被党中央、国务院授予"改革先锋"称号和奖章,被誉为"经济体制改革的积极倡导者"。

在厉以宁先生撰写的皇皇巨著中,除了《中国经济改革发展之路》,厉先生还对《非均衡的中国经济》和《超越政府与超越市场——论道德力量在经济中的作用》两部著作颇为珍视。我向厉先生表态:"您有这个心愿,我一定努力做好另外两部书的英译出版,让国外读者能读到您英文版的三部曲。"

早在改革开放初期,厉以宁先生就提出用股份制改造中国经济的理论,被理论界和政策制定者广泛接受和采纳。在比较研究中国和其他国家经济的基础上,他发展了"非均衡经济理论",并运用这一理论解释中国经济的运行,得到国内外学术界的高度认可。《非均衡的中国经济》一书,就是厉以宁先生首次对中国经济发展"非均衡经济理论"的系统阐述。中国经济改革发展的成功实践,证明了《非均衡的中国经济》一书蕴藏的深刻的思想理论价值。《非均衡的中国经济》1998年被评为"影响新中国经济建设的10本经济学著作",2009年入选"中国文库·新中国60周年特辑",厉以宁先生也因为本书的贡献荣获"2009中国经济理论创新奖"。

在《非均衡的中国经济》中,厉以宁先生从中国的非均衡经济现实着手,以说明资源配置失调、产业结构扭曲、制度创新变型等现象的深层次原因,并进而合乎逻辑地提出中国经济改革必须构建具有充分活力的微观经济主体的政策主张。这部著作是厉以宁先生对于非均衡理论的重要发展和突破,也是其全部所有制改革理论的根基所在,厉先生的所有制改革优先理论和资源配置理论都是非均衡理论的合乎逻辑的延伸和拓展。正是在这个意义上,非均衡理论对中国四十年的经济改革影响深远。

经济学家亚当·斯密为世人所熟知的是其经典著作《国

富论》,他在其中提出了"看不见的手"这一概念,对市场在经济资源配置中的基础性作用做了深刻的探讨。但这只是亚当·斯密的一面,他还撰写了另外一部著名的伦理学著作《道德情操论》。世人大多记住了《国富论》,而对《道德情操论》却知之甚少。然而唯有把这两者放在一起考量,才能帮助我们理解一个完整的亚当·斯密。无独有偶,厉以宁先生不但活跃在中国经济体制改革的前沿,撰写大量经济体制改革的著述,还以经济学家的视角来剖析习惯和道德在经济领域发挥的重大作用。《超越市场与超越政府》凝聚了厉以宁先生这方面的思考。

在《超越市场与超越政府》一书中,厉以宁先生首次将经济学的关注焦点由传统的交易领域引向非交易领域,引向对习惯与道德这一不可替代的第三种调节的重视。针对这个社会与经济生活中日益重要的问题,厉以宁教授以哲人的思辨和学者的笔触,从经济学与哲学视角,对习惯与道德在经济中的调节作用进行了深入论述。作为超越市场调节与政府调节的第三种调节,由习惯力量或道德力量进行的调节在社会经济生活中的作用越来越突出。即使在市场经济中,习惯与道德调节不仅存在着,而且它的作用是市场调节与政府调节所替代不了的。厉先生不是从伦理学家角度来讨论道德和习惯问题,而是把习惯与道德问题纳入经济学的框架中加以研究。对社会经济生活中习惯与道德调节的研究,厉以宁先生堪称首开先河者。

这部《超越市场与超越政府》，连同厉以宁先生的其他经济学论著一道，体现了一个真正的经济学家所应具有的终极关怀，并直指经济学研究的本质。海外有学者将厉以宁先生誉为中国的亚当·斯密，就《中国经济改革发展之路》《非均衡的中国经济》《超越市场与超越政府》这三部代表作而言，我想，厉以宁先生是当之无愧的。

四

在《中国经济改革发展之路》英译本由外研社和剑桥大学出版社联合出版之后，我又主持《非均衡的中国经济》与《超越市场与超越政府》两部著作的英译工作，并就其海外出版与施普林格出版集团商洽合作。施普林格（Springer）是世界第一大科技和医学出版机构，它的logo是国际象棋中骑士的形象，彼时对出版中国主题的人文社科经典学术作品颇为看重。施普林格负责选题的资深编辑李琰女士是北大九七级社会学系学姐，我和李琰学姐就由外研社与施普林格合作出版厉以宁先生这两部著作的英译本很快达成共识。我们也继而想到，在这个合作的基础上，能不能扩展为策划一套以中华优秀传统文化研究和当代中国人文社科研究为主题的学术文库？这个想法也得到了双方高层的肯定。

我们很快发起了外研社·施普林格"中华学术文库"英文丛书的筹备工作。曾担任中共中央政治局常委、国务院副总理的李岚清首长对文库非常重视，还专门为文库篆印作为logo。我们也邀请厉以宁先生担任文库的学术委员，厉先生对此欣然同意。

2012年8月29日，外研社·施普林格"中华学术文库"英文丛书正式启动。厉以宁先生与汤一介先生、乐黛云先生、陆学艺先生等诸位贤哲以耄耋之龄莅临现场并讲话，给我们莫大的鼓舞。我们这套丛书对标的是商务印书馆策划翻译出版的《汉译世界学术名著》丛书。《汉译世界学术名著》丛书把各个学科的世界学术名著介绍给中国读者，开启民智，馨香长存，是当代中国学术史和出版史上的里程碑。

我们有这样的期许和愿景，就是希望外研社·施普林格"中华学术文库"英文丛书能够与《汉译世界学术名著》比肩，成为在中外文明互鉴交流方面的出版"双璧"，以开阔的学术视野和敏锐的学术意识，把中华优秀传统文化和现当代中国研究最有代表性的学术经典以英文的形式介绍给全世界读者，帮助世界读者了解和认识一个历史悠久、文化灿烂的历史中国，了解和认识一个改革开放、和平发展的当代中国。时至今日，外研社·施普林格"中华学术文库"英文丛书已出版著作38种，初具气象，没有辜负厉以宁先生等前贤的厚爱和期望。

五

中国读者有幸,世界读者有幸。

厉以宁先生以经济学理论阐释中国道路的学术著作,越来越多地被译成外文。迄今为止,由外研社译介的厉以宁先生经济学著作外文版已初具规模。《中国经济改革发展之路》《非均衡的中国经济》《超越市场与超越政府》在成功出版英译版之后,相继输出《中国经济改革发展之路》的塞尔维亚语、西班牙语、阿尔巴尼亚语、法语、保加利亚语版本和《超越市场与超越政府》的西班牙语和日语版本。

厉以宁先生这三部代表性的经济学著作译成外文之后,在国外产生了深远的影响。2015年12月14日,哈萨克斯坦总理卡里姆·马西莫夫、第一副总理巴赫特江·萨金塔耶夫一行访问北大光华管理学院,就中哈经济发展合作、中国经济转型与改革和"一带一路"等议题与厉以宁先生进行了深入的交流。马西莫夫总理曾在中国留学,是个"中国通"。没想到马西莫夫总理还是厉以宁先生的超级粉丝,一见面就拿出厉先生《中国经济改革发展之路》与《非均衡的中国经济》的英译版请先生签名,说曾反复研读,并受益匪浅。

为什么厉以宁先生的著作在国外读者中也深受欢迎?我想这与厉先生渊博的知识、深厚的学养、严谨的学风和对现实问题的关切密不可分。厉先生早年在北大求学的时候,陈振汉教授就谆谆教导:要想在经济学研究中取得成就,必须在经济理论、统计、经济史三个方面打好基础。厉以宁先生从负笈北大开始，就像海绵吸水一样如饥似渴地学习，系统研读马克思、哈耶克、兰格、凡勃仑、康芒斯、马歇尔、韦伯、熊彼特、凯恩斯等学者的著作。

厉先生1955年大学毕业留校工作，曾创作词作《鹧鸪天》自勉：

> 溪水清清下石沟，千弯百折不回头。兼容并蓄终宽阔，若谷虚怀鱼自游。　心寂寂，念休休，沉沙无意却成洲。一生治学当如此，只计耕耘莫问收。

厉以宁先生在北大经济系资料室埋头工作二十多年。他践行了词作里的志向，转益多师，兼收并蓄，在深入研习的基础上，翻译了外国经济史的多本著作，还撰写了关于希腊罗马拜占庭经济史的专著。厉先生数十年对外国经济史和西方经济学理论用功颇深，但他并非"言必称希腊"之辈，相反以高度的文化自觉和对中国现实问题的关切，形成系统的思考和研究。

厉以宁先生作为中国经济改革进程的重要亲历者与国有企业股份制改革理论的提出者，对中国改革开放的历程具有深刻的见解。他那些在不同程度上推动了改革的演讲和论文则是对历史转折处最生动直观地描述。厉以宁先生的经济学著作将有助外国读者对中国经济改革的发展路径和内在逻辑拥有更为清晰的理解和参考。正如厉先生2012年在剑桥大学版《中国经济改革发展之路》新书发布会上所做的主旨演讲中所总结的，中国改革开放以来的经济转型是一个双重转型的轨迹——从传统农业社会向工业社会、现代社会的转型，从计划经济体制向市场经济体制的转型。相信国外学界从厉先生"中国道路""双重转型"等充满智慧的理论创见中也会深受启发。

抚今追昔，距严几道先生将亚当·斯密《国富论》译成《原富》在中文世界流布，已将近两个甲子的光景。在这两个甲子的时间里，伴随着中国的富强和复兴，更多具有中国气派、中国气象的经典学术作品也走向世界，为全球治理提供中国方案和中国智慧，产生世界性的影响。

2012年，我随厉以宁先生、何玉春师母和车耳学长访问英国爱丁堡时，曾专门寻访亚当·斯密故居，并合影留念。这真是一张具有历史意义的合影。厉以宁与亚当·斯密的相知相遇，是对两个甲子中中西学术文化交流的极好注解。我想起了厉以宁先生1984年的词作《菩萨蛮·黄山归来》：

隔山犹有青山在，彩云更在群山外。寻路到云边，山高亦等闲。　问君何所志，纵论人间事。寄愿笔生花，香飘亿万家。

六

厉以宁先生青年时期即从事诗词创作,他的诗词作品清新质朴,别开生面。我特别喜欢厉先生那些治史论学、饱含哲理的词作,还曾腼颜请先生亲手题写了三幅词作收藏。转眼即是厉先生九秩寿辰,我挑选了先生一百零八首诗词作品,请资深翻译彭琳女士翻译成英文,计划在先生寿辰之日出版。把准备英译的厉先生诗词数量定在一百零八首,亦有"何止于米,相期于茶"的美好祝福。

中国古典传统对何以长寿有着不同的解读。儒家讲"仁者寿"。子曰:"智者乐水,仁者乐山。知者动,仁者静。知者乐,仁者寿。"(《论语·雍也篇》)道家讲"烟云供养"。明代书画家陈继儒感慨:"黄大痴九十而貌如童颜,米友仁八十余神明不衰,无疾而逝,盖画中烟云供养也。"(《妮古录》卷三)黄公望、米友仁笔下的富春山居、米家山水一派道家气象,甚至黄公望本人也是不折不扣的全真道士。陈继儒认为黄公望、米友仁的长寿,是因为他们常常作画山水,烟岚云岫荡涤心胸。

我觉得儒家和道家二者的说法都可以解释厉以宁先生的长寿。厉先生关切民生、关心民瘼,在重大历史转折关头践行知识分子的时代使命,是真真切切的儒家,"仁者寿"三个大字对厉先生而言是完全匹配的。

厉先生还寄情山水,胸中自有丘壑,他诗词里的每一道山每一条河都灵动着真情和哲思。以"烟云供养"来形容厉先生的胸怀自然恰如其分。前些日子,就厉先生诗词英译出版事,我专程去府上拜望先生。厉先生泡了一杯猴魁绿茶在家等候。何师母说厉先生就喜欢而且一直都喝我家乡黄山的猴魁绿茶。我想起西南联大的一代哲人都喜欢喝茶。汪曾祺先生《泡茶馆》一文探讨了泡茶馆对联大学生有些什么影响。答案是:可以养其浩然之气,保持绿意葱茏的幽默感,战胜恶浊和穷困。我来自徽州茶乡,酷爱喝茶,在人生最困顿的时候曾反复默念汪曾祺先生的这段话,"吾养吾浩然之气","保持绿意葱茏的幽默感",云云。茶客与茶人有所不同,前者是消费者,后者可以是制茶者,但更是精神上的爱茶者。从这个意义上说,汪曾祺先生是茶人,我曾亲炙教诲的赵宝煦先生是茶人,厉以宁先生亦是这样的茶人。茶人胸中自有丘壑,葆有绿意葱茏的幽默感。真正好茶所生发之处,必然是高山之巅、烟云供养。

如何儒道兼济?朱光潜先生"以出世的精神做入世的事业"之语甚得我心。我曾创造性地把四条河流组成一个短语——"洙泗濠濮",来诠释这个含义。

"洙泗",即洙水和泗水,洙水在北,泗水在南,春秋时在鲁国地界。孔子曾于洙泗二水之间讲学,后世因此以洙泗代指孔子教泽,譬如"海滨洙泗""潇湘洙泗"皆此种含义。

"濠濮",即濠水和濮水。《庄子·秋水》中有关于濠水和濮水的两则富有哲思的故事。一则是庄子与惠子濠上观鱼。"子非鱼,安知鱼之乐?""子非我,安知我不知鱼之乐?"这组洋溢着辩证法光辉的对话即出于此。另一则故事是写庄子在濮水边钓鱼,楚王派使者来请庄子去做官。庄子以神龟作喻,向使者发问:"宁其死为留骨而贵乎?宁其生而曳尾于涂中乎?"众人的选择皆是"吾将曳尾于涂中"。后世往往将濠濮并列,寄托庄子《南华经》中遗世高蹈的情怀。北海公园的"濠濮间"与颐和园谐趣园中的"知鱼桥"等都出自"濠濮"的典故。

我一直倾慕朱光潜先生"以出世的精神做入世的事业"之风骨,把"洙泗"和"濠濮"视为志趣的两端,也正因此把书斋陋室取名为"洙泗濠濮"四水堂。洙水泗水濠水濮水四条河流,恰如我徽州老宅之四水归明堂。今年春节,我以"洙泗濠濮"和"松柏桐椿"为镜像自撰联:"闻鹧鸪,熟读稼轩,歌洙泗濠濮;打草稿,搜尽奇峰,写松柏桐椿。"我突然发现这副对联完全可以献给厉以宁先生,暗合了先生左手作诗填词、右手写经世济民论著的旨趣。厉先生的词作颇类稼轩,多阕《鹧鸪天》余音绕梁,洙泗濠濮是先生风范。厉先生做经济学研究,特别注重田野调查,在耄耋之年仍坚持深入中国经济改革第一线去获取第一手信息,从这个角度而言,他与"搜尽奇峰打草稿"的石涛苦瓜和尚是旷代知音。"松柏桐椿"取"松柏同春"之义,古人常以此为题入画,寄托寿庆祝福和美好愿望,沈周、文徵明、八大山人、吴历等皆有《松柏桐椿图》传世。厉先生关切贫困地区的发展,贵州毕节地区的脱贫凝聚着先生数十年的心血——正如先生2012年第七次赴毕节扶贫时创作的词作《踏莎行》:"积雪消融,山林甦醒,纵横百里黄花影。杜鹃绽放漫坡红,春风已过乌蒙岭"——先生为毕节扶贫攻坚一点一滴的进步而惊喜,松柏桐椿是包括毕节在内的中国广大地区经济改革成就的写照,是先生诗意人生的写照。

"当一条河伴随着你成长时,或许它的水声会陪伴你一生。"这是美国作家安·兹温格作品《奔腾的河流》中的名句,出自自然文学研究学者程虹教授的译笔。我非常喜欢这句译文。洙泗濠濮就是流淌在我心灵深处的四条河流,我能感受到它们的涓涓细流和滚滚奔腾。我读厉以宁先生的诗词,也经常会升腾起"洙泗濠濮"之感,先生精彩的词作常有水声相伴。比如,1968年作于昌平北太平庄的《破阵子》:"既是三江春汛到,不信孤村独自寒,花开转瞬间",东坡稼轩的豪气力透纸背。

我最喜欢厉先生1987年的词作《踏莎行》,先生彼时在北京大学图书馆整理手稿《非均衡的中国经济》,赋词抒怀:

> 戒律清规,闲人流语,随风吹过身边去。藏书楼里作忙人,楼高那管花飞絮。 不计浮华,但求警句,愿将心血其中聚。清清流水出深山,须经沙石千回滤。

谨以此文献给厉以宁先生九秩寿辰。